THE URN CARRIER

CHRIS CONVISSOR

THE URN CARRIER

Bink Books
Bedazzled Ink Publishing Company • Fairfield, California

978-1-943837-38-0 paperback
978-1-943837-39-7 epub
978-1-943837-89-2 mobi

Cover Design
by

LS
DESIGNS

Bink Books
a division of
Bedazzled Ink Publishing, LLC
Fairfield, California
http://www.bedazzledink.com

To all my ancestors, my relatives, my siblings and most especially my mother, Margaret and my father, Larry. Without you, I would not be me.

To a certain nineteen-year old: Thank you so much for your integrity, honesty and unflinching courage. I love you without condition. None of this would have happened without your wisdom, drive and generosity.

ACKNOWLEDGMENTS

My gratitude to Claudia Wilde and C.A. Casey for taking a chance on me. Casey, your editing is invaluable. Thank you.

Lynn Starner, thank you for your stunning cover design. Elizabeth Price of Priceless Photography for the Author head shot, you are terrific and we always laugh!

My appreciation and love to:

Holly Bender

My Family

Carolyn Schwab

Jackie and Nancy Ferguson

The Tally Hoes: Jen, Carolyn, Linda, Kathy, Beth, Renee, you women rock!

My Golden Crown Academy classmates, faculty, and staff. Additionally, my appreciation to Ali Sandler, Braxton Busser, Linda Kay Silva, Amanda Kyle Williams, Doug Stanton.

Lee Lynch and Ann McMan, thank you so much for your mentorship through the Academy. You are two of the most incredibly warm and generous people I know.

"No matter where I am, and even if I have no clear idea where I am, and no matter how much trouble I may be in, I can achieve a blank and shining serenity if only I can reach the very edge of a natural body of water. The very edge of anything from a rivulet to an ocean says to me;' Now you know where you are. Now you know which way to go. You will soon be home now."

—Kurt Vonnegut

"If I take the wings of the morning and dwell in the uttermost parts of the Sea, even then Thine hand would lead me and Thy right hand envelope me."

—Psalm 139

PROLOGUE

TESSA HAD DONE a face plant in snow. She couldn't move. She felt the cold snow on the left side of her face and neck. The heat from her jugular pounded a space with every heartbeat between her skin and the snow. She counted her heartbeats—one, two, three, four.

Someone else was breathing in her ear.

"Tessa!" Her twin brother, Eli, was bending over her. "Please. Get up. Don't be dead."

Dead? A rocketing explosion in her head, and in her gut, propelled her to twist and look up, but her eyes wouldn't focus, so she had this blurry thing going on, like she had put on some old person's thick glasses. She squeezed her eyes as tight as she could and counted one, two, three, four before letting them open again. Bare tree limbs high up seemed to be clearer.

"Oh God, Tessa." Eli pulled her to her knees and held her. Her face was matted with something. Gooey, warm, mud? She tasted blood in her mouth.

Eli was sobbing like a little boy, not an almost man.

He was clutching her so hard his fingers were digging into her spine through her wool jacket. She was frightened by his sobs rocketing off the hills in these remote woods and she wondered why were they kneeling on this incline and why her stomach and head hurt so much? In the distance she heard a truck lumbering, wheeling, and whining down the old two-track. Forward it drove and then reversed. The engine plunged and shifted and roared, ramming and pushing through the thick snow on the Rayle road. Even though the hills were thawing, the snowmobilers had padded down a track on the seasonal road all winter long. It was very near impossible to get through.

In fact, her dad and Eli and she had snowshoed in on the road from 669. Her dad.

She doubled over, her insides cramping. A three-pronged bird claw twisting inside her.

"Oh fuck, Eli, what's going on?"

She felt like her insides were tumbling out. Because they were.

CHAPTER 1

Three Years Later

AS ASHES GO, Aunt Sadie hardly amounted to two cottage cheese containers. Tessa's neighbors' St. Bernard had required a shoebox.

The gold filigree vase, Aunt Sadie's last container, sits on a beautiful dark, delicate mahogany wood table. The urn is perfectly centered on a small veil of Hungarian lace in a circle just like the tabletop. Various relatives mill around, scarcely giving the urn or the table a glance as they look at other furniture, dishes, ornaments, silverware, glassware, the keepsakes, the things on the wall, all to be divided. Aunt Sadie never had any kids of her own.

Tessa lounges against the wall, her brown-and-pink hair, with a shock of blonde in the middle, draped over one eye. Although Tessa probably hadn't met Great Aunt Sadie more than two or three times, she'd been totally enamored by her.

At family gatherings, Great Aunt Sadie hung out with all the kids. She didn't stand much taller than their eight-, nine-, ten-year-old selves. She always wore brightly colored pantsuits, like sunflower yellows and fuchsia pinks and eye-popping lime greens. She wore gold jangly things around her waist and would gyrate impressively, the bells and clangy things making tinkling water noises. Sort of like when the snow would melt off the roof and run into the gutters. Aunt Sadie claimed she was a belly dancer.

Uncle Percy, her husband, had been just the opposite of Sadie. He had been super tall. He never said much. Everyone said he was Canadian. Tessa figured that meant Canadians didn't talk much.

He'd stand, leaning one shoulder against the wall, impressive with his shock of white, thick, well-groomed hair, smiling. His bright turquoise blue eyes grinned when he watched his wife belly dance—holding her hands out to the children, engaging them in dancing with her, encouraging them to mimic her moves, fluttering around like a happy sparrow in spring. Diminutive sprite fit her perfectly. Uncle Percy would watch with a big grin. The smile they shared in their eyes as they'd wink at each other would provoke Aunt Sadie to say, "He's my forever love!"

Tessa wanted a love like Uncle Percy and Aunt Sadie's.

Aunt Sadie never talked down to the children. Even though she was old and wrinkly, she'd sit at the kids' table during meals and share secret jokes about all the adults. Aunt Deidre positively hated it when Aunt Sadie would sit with the kids.

Most of the time, Sadie and Percy lived in Florida. The last time Tessa saw Great Aunt Sadie, Percy had died the year before. But instead of being all sad and gloomy, Sadie enthralled the kids at dinner with ghost stories about how Percy returned the day Aunt Deidre came over to this very country house.

"She was telling me I had to move in with her and Chuck," Aunt Sadie whispered as they sat at the kids table. "No offense to you two." She motioned to Jill and Joe, Deidre and Chuck's kids, before continuing her dramatic replay. "Well. Percy was having none of that. The garage door started going up and down. It did it four times. All by itself."

"Maybe a plane flew over and set it off?" Eli suggested.

"Four times?" Aunt Sadie asked. "Then, when she told me I had to sell the house, well, that did it. The lights started coming on and off. She had the nerve to ask *me* what was wrong. I just said, plain and simple, 'Percy doesn't like you.' But do you think that stopped her?" Aunt Sadie's fork was midair.

She waited for all the kids to shake their heads.

"No. She followed me into the kitchen. And when she bent over to look at what I was cooking in the oven, well," Sadie paused for effect, "don't you know that refrigerator door flies open and smacks her right in the ass."

The kids' eyes widened, and they all laughed so hard, Eli's milk came out his nose. Then they all laughed together about that. No one said swear words in conversational tone to them but Aunt Sadie.

"That's when I said, 'I think Percy is telling you to leave.'"

All the kids shivered and agreed: it had to be Uncle Percy. Aunt Sadie wasn't done. In a stage whisper loud enough for all the adults at the grown-up table in the next room to hear she said, "She's just after my money. She's got a looooooooooooong wait coming."

Aunt Sadie was like a kid but a lot older.

"Why do you sit with us?" Tessa asked. "When you can sit at the big table?"

"Well, sweetie, it's like this. At these family gatherings, I much prefer your company."

That was twelve years ago. Aunt Sadie never did sell the country house, but she got as far away from Aunt Deidre and Uncle Chuck as she could. She remained in Florida.

Tessa finds it odd the dining room table has been moved to the living room. All that remains in the dining room are the tiny table and the vase. She watches all the adults and some of the cousins printing their initials on little labels and sticking them on all the material things they want. She sighs and wanders into the large old farm kitchen. She hops onto one of the counters and scrounges a chocolate chip cookie from a nearby platter before Jill unceremoniously pushes open the heavy swinging kitchen door.

"Thought I'd find you here." Jill smirks, her forearm deep into the potato chip bag. She munches like a cow grazing in a field, her eyes scanning the shelves for anything of value. The same zombie look everyone has outside the kitchen. Jill wanders over to the oven and looks inside.

Tessa watches the refrigerator door, and by the fourth count, it doesn't even hint at moving. She glances out the large window behind her. Murphy, the black, flat-coat retriever, is sniffing in the melting snow, wandering from fence side to fence side. Tessa wonders if he knows his owner is in the vase.

"This is so lame." Jill is trying to engage Tessa in camaraderie talk, like they are the cool ones of the group and everyone else just side characters. "How long do you think it's going to take?"

Tessa shrugs, keeping her silence. She doesn't dislike Jill, she just doesn't get her. Jill makes her uncomfortable. She is classically pretty, with large almond eyes and dark hair, a bit heavy, with an attitude a mile long. She is loud, assumptive, and sometimes shares too much information, like now.

"That date I went on last night? Totally a waste. The guy didn't even try to kiss me. Just wanted me to blow him. Like, really? Are you serious, dude?" Jill half laughs.

Ewwww. Tessa tries to not focus on the potato chip remnants hanging from the corner of Jill's mouth, but it's kinda hard to look away. Jill's presence demands you pay attention to her before she can . . . *uh oh.*

"That guy you were chatting up at the bar seemed pretty cool."

Yup. Jill was that intrusive. They haven't seen each other in five years, and now here they are, at Aunt Sadie's wake, and all of a sudden they are supposed to share their deepest, darkest secrets.

Tessa just shakes her head.

"I mean, how does that work anyway?"

"Tessa!" Her mom's voice from the dining room rescues her.

Tessa scoots off the counter. She starts to toss the half a chocolate chip cookie in the waste basket, and Jill's hand intercedes.

"If you're not going to eat that, I will," Jill says. "May as well not go to waste. You don't have any infectious diseases, right? I'm just kidding, man. Geez, don't look like death just walked in."

Tessa hands over the last half of the cookie as her mom pushes open the door, revealing a crowd in the dining room.

"We need you." The lines between her mom's eyes seem deeper than normal and the dark circles under her eyes even darker.

Tessa follows her mom into the dining room and all the relatives are looking at her. An old man she has never seen before, appraises her carefully from head to toe. He has large round glasses, and his crinkly wrinkly eyes are an unreadable watery blue. He looks stern. Even though he is old, something about him makes Tessa's skin crawl. It's almost as if he knows everything about her, about Eli, about . . .

"Well, Beth, tell her." Aunt Deidre's voice kills her thoughts.

Her mom's nervous tic, a quick head shake, jumps through Tessa's energy. Her mom is really upset, but trying to keep it together.

"I don't know how to say this Tessa . . ." Her mom looks at the old man.

The old man clears his throat. "Tessa, is it?" He waits for her to acknowledge him with a nod.

"I am Dan Forsythe, your Great Aunt Sadie's lawyer. Her will is very specific. Before any of her monies, trust, and personal belongings are disbursed, her ashes must be spread in various locations, on a specific route."

His cough rattles shallowly from his throat, and not from his chest. To Tessa, his throat resembles a turkey's waddle. Why she is so fixated on people's appearances today mystifies her. Maybe she always notices these things, but today, for some reason, she is acutely aware of them. She realizes he's been speaking and catches up with his words.

"And in accordance with her wishes someone must scatter these ashes in a certain order. It's not a difficult task. It seems like no one has an open schedule but you."

Tessa opens her mouth and then closes it. Her mom stands next to her, not looking at her but at the floor, and touches her forearm.

"I told them that just because you are in between jobs and are unsure if you're going to return to school next semester, didn't mean you were available," she says, her quiet voice painfully etching out her words. "In fact, I said you were unavailable."

"Whoa, dude," Jill says from behind her, catching the drift far faster than Tessa. "I can't do it. I'm in pre-med."

"That's what I told them." Aunt Deidre's exasperation annunciated through her arms flinging out to the side.

Fourteen relatives shift on their feet uncomfortably as they looked expectantly at Tessa. Uncle Chuck, front and center, crosses his arms across his large, girthy belly. He looks like a horse that swallowed a hippo.

"You don't have a job. Well, you do now."

He starts to light the half stale, stinky cigar he has in his hand.

The lawyer glares at him. "There'll be none of that."

Everyone looks at him, but the lawyer is unmistakably speaking to Chuck.

"Not in the house." The lawyer's stare lasers into Chuck so hard the energy in the room vibrates. The static is palatable.

Chuck scowls, releasing the flame on the lighter. He jams the unlit cigar in his mouth. He chomps on it as if he is chewing steel. His eyes narrow, exposing a molten anger beneath Chuck's otherwise fluffy exterior.

Tessa looks at the urn. What the hell?

"Before anything is removed from the house," the creepy dude says to Tessa in a much calmer voice, "before monies are . . ."

She holds up her hand. She gets it. She looks at him directly. "What about Murphy?"

A slight upturn on the old guy's thin blue lips, reveals his amusement.

"The dog?" Aunt Deidre asks. "You're worried about the dog? Isn't he like, a hundred years old?"

"Excellent question." The lawyer looks at his papers. "Your Aunt Sadie wants Murphy to go along."

"That cinches it," Jill says. "I'm allergic to dogs."

More like allergic to doing anything for anybody else.

Tessa laughs, and then frowns. She knows she heard a voice, but apparently no one else has. It's unlike her to be that sarcastic.

"Something funny?" the lawyer asks.

No. I'm sorry. I—"

"You don't have to apologize," her mom says. "This is ridiculous. She's been put on the spot by all of you. Wanting things."

Her mom despises greed. She told Tessa she was dreading seeing the relatives today, fussing over Aunt Sadie's things. The only reason Tessa agreed to come was because she could see how upset her mom was. And her mom always stood by her. It was the least she could do.

"Mom. Let me think a moment. I'm not sure I understand everything."

"Why don't you all get refreshments?" the lawyer says to everyone else. "While Tessa and her mom and I find a quiet room to discuss the details."

"Wow, better you than me," Jill whispers to Tessa, before returning to the kitchen.

Once the lawyer details everything, Tessa fully understands why no one else is willing to undertake the task.

"So let me get this straight." Tessa is sitting on the edge of the comfortable bed. It's a bright room, with older dark furniture and light flowing in through airy windows. Light walls. Old-fashioned. Her mom sits beside her. Murphy at her feet.

"Aunt Sadie wants some ashes in Lake Superior, Lake Michigan, and then I start driving to various places across the US and Canada and spill some of her ashes out? Then I call you each time, check in, and when all her ashes are gone, I return? And it's all paid for? Do we know how long it might take?"

"About three months. You could do it sooner, but there is no need to rush. Whoever does it is welcome to take her 1968 truck and the camper. Then Murphy can go with you. I'll give you sufficient funds to make the first third of the trip and then dispense funds as you need till you finish."

He reaches in his pocket and hands her the very newest iPhone.

"It's all paid for. Your Aunt Sadie is very detailed about the route. Your mom has suggested that along the way you might want to visit some family friends? Or whomever?" He looks at Mom.

"I just thought, if you are indeed going to do this for the family, that there might be some places you'd like to go too, since you will be near. Like Uncle Mark and Dolly's."

Uncle Mark really isn't her uncle. He's a best friend of her mom's. He taught Tessa how to fly a single engine

Cessna 170 when she was fourteen. He even coached her through landing the tail wheeled vehicle and marveled at her natural abilities. Uncle Mark and Aunt Dolly had moved to an airplane community in Florida. She'd never been. That would be fun to see.

Murphy sighs. As uneasy as she feels with the lawyer, Tessa loves Murphy on sight. Murphy is totally bonding with her. He is following her everywhere.

The lawyer looks at Murphy and Tessa. "You do seem the natural choice."

Tessa pets Murphy. "I'll do it."

"I'm glad to hear that."

The lawyer glances behind himself once, and then backs up a step. He shuffles his papers. Tessa and her mom share a curious look and shrug. The guy is blocking the door, they have to wait. Murphy licks his non-existent balls.

"If you successfully complete the task as written, your college tuition is paid in full."

Tessa's mouth drops open.

"Excuse me?" her mom asks, her hand to her heart, as if she is about to faint. "I didn't think Aunt Sadie . . . I mean . . . She seemed to live hand to mouth."

Just like us. Tessa could hear her mom's unsaid words.

"Ahhh. Seemed." The lawyer nods. He looks up. "Yes, well. It's what her instructions say. Tessa accepts the task, she finishes it, and Sadie agrees to pay her tuition in full."

He speaks as if Great Aunt Sadie is still alive.

"I know some of the male relatives asked about her truck and trailer; however, those are already off premises being updated for your future road trip," he continues. "New tires, oil change, gone over so you won't have any trouble. The interior of the camper is being cleaned, updated, and readied. Stocked for the first leg of your trip. Can you leave in a month?"

Tessa nods.

"Good. It's settled then?"

The hardest part for Tessa is shaking the old man's frigid, cold hand.

BEFORE THEY LEAVE the wake, Tessa takes Murphy out back one last time. Over the door to the backyard is an industrial sticker. The kind posted at the front of orchards, or maybe where there is asbestos in the area. It reads: "Enter at Your Own Risk" in bright red letters. Aunt Sadie has all sorts of cool stuff stuck everywhere. An artificial walnut with an animated fake spider was in a nut bowl. It made Jill scream.

As Tessa hits the bottom step, a dark figure moves swiftly from her left. Before she knows it she's crouched into a defensive posture with her hands balled up in front of her, ready to throw punches.

"Whoa, dude." Her cousin Joe laughs. "You'd never be able to take me."

But Murphy is right there, his flag-like tail up and his body between them. Joe looks down and backs up a step.

"Easy there, I was just gonna offer you a hit." Joe shows her a lit joint and looks around the corner of the house to make sure no one inside can see them.

Tessa shakes her head. "I have to drive. Mom's beat."

"Yeah, that was one hell of an exciting episode in there. Sorry 'bout the old man," Joe says of his dad.

Tessa waves him off. "He's just always pissed at me."

"Yeah. He blames you for everything."

This is not news. She's used to being people's whipping post. She wonders if it's because she never hits back. She doesn't want to become like the people attacking her, so she defers her responses. She takes it out in her running. She pets Murphy reassuringly and he goes off to do his business.

"Mom and Dad are dickheads. Aunt Sadie nailed that one. Forget about them. You and Eli have always been my favorite cousins." Joe stubs out the joint on the fading grey of the cedar siding. "If I wasn't in nursing school, I'd take the gig."

Tessa is strangely protective of the house and Joe sees her look at the smudge. He wipes it clean with a thumb. His hands are large. His thumb would probably cover half her palm. Cousin Joe has become quite handsome. Standing six-four, he has the Jesus look all the girls fall for—the moustache, beard, the shoulder-length brown hair, the high cheekbones that run in their family and he has incredibly bright inquisitive brown eyes.

"How's Eli doing anyway?"

"He's okay."

"You going to see him on your way north?"

"Yeah," Tessa conceded. "If I can."

"That's where you gotta go first, right? North?"

"How'd you know?"

"Oh." Joe waves a hand dismissively, as if it isn't important.

Murphy rejoins them, this time sitting squarely in front of Tessa, facing Joe.

"Mom. She gets all the details," Joe finally says. He stoops to pet Murphy, but Murphy moves his head.

"Guess he isn't real affectionate, huh? Not like Aunt Sadie, she was one of a kind."

Tessa doesn't know what to say.

"So why are you doing this?" Joe asks.

"I dunno. I'm sick of school. I want a break. Why not?"

"Cool. I get it. Take a break. Road trip. Whatever."

Tessa nods.

"Well, I best make an appearance before Dad comes around the corner." Joe reaches out to hug her but Murphy is immovable, so he clumsily touches her half on the shoulder. "Be cool, cuz." He jogs up the back steps.

Tessa looks down at Murphy, once the door closes Joe inside.

"You really don't like him, do you?"

Murphy looks up at her and wags his tail against her leg, one, two, three, four times.

They were going to get along just fine.

CHAPTER 2

Eighteen months earlier.

TESSA WAS ON a gurney, surrounded by the privacy drape. Waiting. A nurse came in and regarded her with a genuine smile.

"Your morning cocktail." She held the syringe upward from her elbow. "Which cheek?"

Tessa rolled to her left and the prick pain of the hypodermic was immediate.

"That will start to settle quickly and everything is in order," the nurse reassured her.

Tessa rolled back and her mom took her hand.

"I am so proud of you," her mom said.

Tessa's eyes filled with tears. "I think I'll be okay. That surgery at sixteen had to be worse, right?"

Her mom nodded.

"That was three layers of muscle, right, so this should be a piece of cake." Already the drug was taking effect. Tessa's fear was fleeing to some recessive bank of clouds. Everything seemed brighter in the room, and lighter. She was exhilarated.

"Oh my God." She smiled. "I am so glad this is happening." It was the last thing she remembered before waking again. A man with dark golden skin above his mask was standing over her, eyes smiling behind his glasses.

"Hi, Tessa, I'm Dr. McMan. I'm your anesthesiologist today. All I need you to do is breathe deeply and count back from one hundred."

Tessa didn't even get to ninety-six.

She remembered the recovery room because there was a

baby crying. From her previous surgeries, when you could read the clock on the wall, they let you go to your room. She asked if she could be moved. The baby's wailing was giving her a headache and making her nauseous. She could hardly see. The attendant asked her to look at the wall and she just made out the time.

"Close enough," he said and started wheeling her out, but wait, the baby was coming too!

It was all Tessa could do to not puke as they rode the elevator together, the crying baby and her. She tried to have empathy for the infant. Why was it here? What surgery did it have to have? She was relieved when they pushed her away from the noise and the racket.

Once in the room, her stomach began to settle. Now the regimen of ice chips. And then there would be the dull ache of pain returning. She remembered the drill. She could handle it.

Her mom was there waiting. Every time she woke, her mom was always right there, reading a book, or just watching her. She grabbed Tessa's hand each time and gave it a reassuring shake.

"I love you," Tessa said and fell asleep for hours.

The burning pain began as a dull ache and inched up toward bonfire status. They kept her in the hospital to make sure she was peeing okay. They wouldn't let her out till she stomached a full meal and she walked down the hallway and back, several times.

She was only slightly sedated now. No more pain shots. She began weaning herself off pain pills. With sedation removed, the burning pain was sharper but her muscles healed faster. She was not bedridden, or foggy. She could see clearly and taste food. The surgeon came in.

"Knees up?" It was not really a question.

She froze at his casual flipping up of the sheet.

"Everything is looking pink. No sign of infection," he said, sounding as if he was down a deep tunnel and relaying the news back to earth. "I couldn't be more pleased."

He flipped the sheet down, patted her gently on the knees, and nodded for her to relax.

He read and wrote in the chart, and typed into the laptop. She liked this hospital. They doubled down on everything, written chart and digital so there were no mistakes.

"You're very strong." He smiled. "Weaning yourself from the pain medication, are you?"

Tessa nodded. He reached down and affectionately held her socked foot.

"I will see you in two weeks at my office." He walked to the door and looked back. "I'm very proud of you."

It took six months before she could run a full quarter mile without stopping. At first, she just walked around the track, once, at Ralph Young Field, MSU. In three months she was fully running part way, taking the quarter mile oval track curve as fast as she could in sprints, her long hair flying. As she hit the straight away she eased up and jogged easily to the outside.

Almost autumn, and the football players were released from the stadium. Some of them stood by the fence.

She didn't really notice the football players at first because lots of folks were jogging and pacing and running. The same group she'd seen, older people, younger people, some athletes. Non-athletes were supposed to run on the outside three lanes, but she considered this elitist. So she did what she wanted as long as she didn't interrupt anyone else's routine. When she did the sprints she took the lane she wanted. When she walked she made her way to the outside. She was on her last two sprints, her long legs running. Her arms pumped, hands open, eyes focused, first on Case Hall, and then the big round curve of the stadium. It was freeing to run so hard. Any pain, any residual burn, dissipated in her running, legs and feet punishing the cushy red surface of the track.

At the fence line, as she finished her last sprint and gently jogged to the outside to slow and then walk, clapping reached her ears and she realized other people were in her world. She saw three or four football players openly admiring her.

"You have some fast feet, girl." It wasn't sexual. It was true admiration.

Tessa felt herself flushing. They high-fived her and turned and walked away—their helmets in their hands, their cleats clacking against the blacktop path.

"You keep working it," one of them called back, and she waved, smiling.

Tessa felt like a rock star.

TESSA HAS A recurring dream involving her mom and her twin brother, Eli. In it they've narrowly escaped a monster. They're running in the woods back of the first home she can remember. A treacherous trail of roots and large trees. It seems like it's October, because they're in Halloween costumes, and it's cold. Tessa has lost a shoe, but her mom is quietly pleading with her to run anyway, so Tessa runs silently, their breathing the only noise.

All of a sudden the monster is in front of them. His face is grotesque and misshapen, as if he too is wearing a Halloween mask, but he isn't. He's growling and bleeding and he swings his arm back and forth.

He has a sharp machete in his right hand, and the monster laughs at them. "Little bits. They'll never find you. No one will ever know."

Each time she wakes from this dream, it's like she's under water. She's inhaling huge gasps of air, as if she hasn't been breathing at all.

ANOTHER DREAM, BUT more like a memory and this one is true, because her grandmother still speaks of it. Tessa was only four or five at the time.

Grandmother had sent for them. She lived in the remote area of Ontario. Between Sioux Lookout and Sudbury, along the rail line was a singular post with a stick on it.

When the stick was up, the train stopped and picked up the pair of Anishinaabe and took them into town for supplies. Heading north out of Minnesota, her mother told the conductor where they needed to stop and he nodded, knowingly.

They looked out the windows until their mom said they were close, and they gathered their packs and put on their shoes again. Her mom ushered them to the front of their car, and the train started slowing, slowing, slowing. Each braking a puzzle to the other passengers looking up from their papers and snacks. What could be the problem in this wilderness? Then they spied the trio in the front and stared.

Each time the train braked, Eli and Tessa swayed into their mother's wool pants and soft coat. It was the color of deer. Then the man in the hat and uniform slid open their car and they dismounted from the black grated steps, their mom helping lift them off.

They moved from the big white sharp rocks and down the slope, and the man leaned way out and waved toward the front of the train. The train started chugging slowly away. Some people waved at them, and Eli and Tessa waved back.

When the train was gone, there they were, in the middle of nowhere with no one around and only the humming of the tracks as it registered the steel wheels long down the line.

In the midst of tall pine and tamarack, was a little footpath to follow. Maybe it was more a wildlife track. They begin the mile long walk to Grandma and Grandpa's house. Tessa loved the smell of pine and tamarack. This was late spring, but not fly season. Still a cold nipped to the air, but the sun was up and full. They trudged alongside their mother, carrying their little backpacks of food. They would wear the same clothes day in and out for the week that they stayed. It was more important to take food, and Senna leaves and greens for her grandmother and grandfather. Her mother sang, "Carry me down the old Piney Road."

Her mother carried the larger pack with all the supplies her adopted mom and dad requested. Fat back, side pork, salt, and coffee, maybe some sweets, honey, and tea. And a fifth of Seagram's V.O for Grandpa. As they walked along the mushy melting snow, her mom suddenly stopped singing and put hands across the chests of Tessa and Eli, as if stopping them from going through the windshield of a car.

In front of them, a large black bear stood, sniffing the air. Sniffing, sniffing. It sank down on all fours and growled and struck a huge paw through the snow, warning. Her mom froze, then, ever so slowly, placed Tessa and Eli around behind her, not taking her eyes off the bear.

The bear stood once more, and sniffed left and sniffed right, grunting, and suddenly two cubs scrambled up on the trail with her. The bear padded a few steps forward and struck her paw through the snow again. Warning. Keeping her cubs close, she huffed and snuffed breaths in, as if reading the air. Then she stopped all movement. Her cubs stayed very still behind her, as if knowing their mom was making a decision.

"Mmmmmmm," the bear seemed to say. At least, that was what Tessa heard. Then the bear turned left and crossed into the pine. There were little noises of the pine brushing against her fur and then nothing.

Their mom remained motionless.

Eli and Tessa looked up at her.

Later she would say a million thoughts went through her head. Should they make a break for it and head back to the rails? Should she drop the packs with all the food and honey and peanut butter?

She stayed rooted, listening, every muscle straining to sense if the bear was still there. Finally, their mom cautiously stepped forward, as if walking along a steep ledge, keeping her twins near and to her left side, away from where the bear had crossed into the pine.

As they stepped into the big melty footprints the bear had left, her mom stopped once more. There, not very far in the pines, was the bear, quietly watching on all fours, her cubs behind her, soundless and motionless.

Silently, her mom pushed Tessa and Eli forward. They continued walking ahead of their mother, her gently pushing them along, her back to them, as she walked backward.

The bear came out, walking on all fours, and then stood once more. She took in one large breath, and dropped down, pushing her cubs ahead of her, treading slowly down the path toward the train tracks, continuing her path from hibernation.

CHAPTER 3

TESSA AND BILLY, her boyfriend, just arrive home from his lacrosse game, and she hears the rumbling of a Harley, or maybe, something larger, coming behind them. A beautiful, butter cream and baby blue pick-up with a matching color-coordinated trailer pulls to the curb of her house.

"Tessa Williams?" A handsome guy, maybe mid-twenties, steps out. His dimples are deep. His eyes green.

She nods.

He brings a digital handheld tracker, the kind like the UPS drivers have, and has her sign on the line. He clips it to his belt and reads from his clipboard. "We need to go over the entire vehicle and make sure it's to your satisfaction."

"Holy shit," Billy says lowly. "This is it? This is what you're driving all over the country and Canada?"

Tessa is having a difficult time controlling her grin.

"Can I go inside?" Billy lifts his chin at the camper, and the delivery guy nods as he unlocks the door.

Billy climbs inside. "Holy freaking shit."

"Don't mind him," Tessa says to the delivery guy. "He lives in a cave."

"Dude, holy crap, flat screen TV."

Tessa has no idea what Billy is rambling about. She is walking with the handsome delivery guy to the front of the truck. His blue uniform name tag says Paul. Paul shows her how to open the engine. She looks at the latch. He shows her again. She does it right the first time.

"Great," he says. And waits a beat as if expecting her to say or do something else. "Okay then."

He reaches an arm in front of her. The engine looks new and shiny.

"Oil stick, there's a gauge inside, but check it every morning after a long haul. Be sure you're on a flat surface when you check it. Here's a niff-noff storage area, for a rag and an extra quart. We put Synthetic Premium blend in. You have any serious problems, you call us first, okay? Card's taped to the inside of the glove compartment door." Paul then shows her the transmission stick, the brake fluid, the antifreeze reservoir, and the windshield washer container.

"Nothing computer on here. Old-fashioned roll-up windows, though we did install an a/c for you, and that back extra hatch on the cab is for the dog. You have two fuel tanks, a saddle," he flips the front seat forward, showing her what she guesses is a gas tank, "And the back one." He taps the driver's side, just behind the cab. "Thirty-five gallons all told. The kayak fits in under the extra cab."

"Kayak?" Tessa squeaks and peers into the bed of the truck where Paul has pointed. A brand new red Perception, with vest and paddle, are tucked neatly corner to corner. "I don't know how to kayak."

"Piece of cake," Billy says, jumping out of the camper. "That is one sweet set up in there. Shower, toilet, kitchen. Sure you don't want me to go with you?"

He rounds the front of the truck and is making his way to her. Paul starts the engine and Billy stops. He turns and lets out a long whistle while putting both hands on each of the front quarter panels. He leans in, absorbing the simplicity and beauty of the engine.

"Dude, that's not a 390 is it?" he asks Paul.

Paul nods with a broad grin.

Great, Tessa thinks, guy talk time.

"That is cherry. Damn, you'd better hope old Aunt whoever is paying the gas for this."

Before Tessa can ask any questions, a black 350 King Rancher pulls in front.

"My ride," Paul explains. "But I have to show you how everything works in the camper. I'll also leave a list of how you set up and tear down. And, if you'd like, we can take some time and go over the basics of backing this thing up. I noticed the parking lot next door, we can practice there."

"I can show her all that, dude." Suddenly Billy seems a little possessive.

Paul shakes his head. "The executor of the will, the lawyer, made it very clear what my obligations are. I have to follow them to the letter of the law, or I don't get paid."

Paul stands a full head taller than Billy, and the way he rolls his work shirt sleeves up past his finely muscled biceps, isn't hard to look at either. She sees them flex just ever so slightly. Either that, or she just wants him to flex them.

"Billy, it's okay." She puts a hand on Billy's forearm. "This is going to take a while, so why don't I call you when we're through?"

"Yeah," Billy agrees, pushing his long locks from his eyes. "Do that. Call me. We'll hit Centre Street café for dinner, k?"

He kisses her, longer than he needs to.

Paul, seemingly totally disinterested, wanders to the back of the trailer.

"Sweet fucking ride." Billy sighs. "Wish I could go."

Paul explains the propane igniter switches and the trailer's water and waste system, and then walks her back to the pickup.

"Hop in, take me for a ride."

"So the lawyer. You meet him?" Tessa asks, trying to take her mind off Paul's arms and dimples while she starts the truck.

Paul nods. "Yeah. He's seriously one scary looking dude isn't he?"

"Totally."

"Kind of creepy," Paul adds.

So it isn't just her.

"I'm gonna leave my cell phone too, cause you're going to be in different time zones. Might be after business hours." He opens the glove compartment and writes his number on the garage business card, left-handed.

Before Tessa can ask anything else, Paul instructs her on trailering and backing, high winds, the anti-sway bar, the electric brake system. All business and details. Tessa's head is going to explode.

"Don't worry, I made up a whole book."

He reaches behind her and taps a binder riding on the back shelf that's supposed to be Murphy's bed. She senses his energy just from his arm being that close.

"Truck and trailer for dummies?" she jokes as she tries backing without swiveling her head.

Paul has told her she must rely on the mirrors, both the big rectangular part, and the little orb convex ones that show everything in miniature. Steer opposite to cock the trailer away, steer same curve to straighten it. When he is sure she is used to the truck and trailer together, he instructs her to back into a car space, even though the parking lot is empty.

"I want to see if you can get it between the lines, perfectly."

She doesn't get it the first time, but with his coaching, they end up laughing and she finally succeeds.

"You're a quick learner," Paul says. "You could get your commercial license and drive the big rigs down the highway."

Tessa grimaces. "No, thank you."

"So how did you get rooked into this?"

She shrugs. "Luck of the Irish." They laugh again because of her dark skin and hair.

"C'mon," he says. "Show me you can back it in your driveway. Just take the road like you own it. Traffic can wait. Drive into the opposite lane so you get the maximum angle you need to do it in one take."

She finally accomplishes not hitting the house or backing over the neighbor's lawn.

"There ya go," he says. "A pro. Hey, I have one more thing to put in that binder. I'll be right back."

He jogs to the big black truck waiting for him and is there a few moments.

She runs her hand along the side of the truck, the shininess and the newness of it. How comfortable it felt to be behind the wheel, like she'd been driving it all her life. She walks alongside the ribbed trailer with the little slatted windows. A small Honda generator had been included for boon docking, whatever that is. She has a lot to read. Paul said there were all sorts of books in the rig under the seats.

He comes up behind her. "All set." Then he smiles. "When is departure?"

"I have another week of school, then I promised my mom I'd visit with her. My lease is up in two weeks."

"So . . . anytime for a drink?" he asks her directly.

"I think I can make some time." She smiles.

HER BEST UNIVERSITY friend in the whole world, Dina, stops by before she has a chance to call Billy.

"Oh my gosh, this is it?" Dina stands a head taller than Tessa. She is slim and blonde with her long hair swaying down her back. She walks with a slight graceful angular walk. Tessa thinks she moves softly, like a crane. Dina would snort and say, "More like a girl with scoliosis."

Dina is peering inside the trailer.

Tessa laughs. "Go on in, it's not going to bite you."

She follows her in. With two of them inside, the trailer seems to suddenly shrink.

Dina spies the queen-size bed and falls on it backward. "Wow, that's even comfortable."

"It has storage underneath."

"I don't care about the storage. Close the trailer door." Dina stretches out her arms, grinning.

Tessa smiles, complies, and slides into Dina's arms.

After they make love, Dina breathes into Tessa's hair, "I wanted to be the first to do that."

"You were the first a long time ago." Tessa's voice feels muffled between Dina's skin and the comforter on the bed. Their clothes are everywhere.

"This place is a mess!"

"Thanks to you."

"Is there a beer in the fridge?" Dina leans over to reach the refrigerator door.

"I don't even know if it is on."

"Oh look. Beer. The good kind."

"No shit?" Maybe that's what Paul left behind.

Dina removes the magnetic bottle opener on the front of the door and pops the beer open, letting the top fly into the middle of the trailer. They laugh. The beer is deliciously cold.

"I'm gonna miss you." Dina pushes a lock of Tessa's hair behind her ear.

"Come with me."

Dina shakes her head as she takes another swig. "No can do. At least now. Maybe later in your trip? When you have to hit British Columbia. That would be fun."

"Could you take that much time, two weeks in Canada with me? Maybe three?"

"Sure, that's a couple months down the road. I'll be free

then. Doesn't Billy want to go?" Dina smiles. Tessa sees a knowing look in her eyes.

"Billy." Tessa sighs and rolls over on her back, her bare breasts exposed. "You know he's sweet, he's just . . ."

"So boring," they say together.

"But you should have seen the delivery guy."

"Someone I need to be jealous about?"

"As if." Tessa shoves Dina, then grabs her blouse off the floor and puts it on.

"As if what?"

"Xander and you."

Dina nods and drinks. "Well, Xander isn't clueless about female parts."

"And he's hot." Tessa takes the beer from Dina.

"He's super-hot, but can he work?" That was Dina, always looking ahead. "I need a steady Eddie. Someone that's going to be there in the long haul."

"Don't we all?"

"Mmm." Dina finishes the beer. "At least we have each other."

CHAPTER 4

TESSA'S BIG MORNING finally arrives. Packing stuff she wants for after the trip and selling or giving away things, becomes a sort of purging, an unexpected cleansing. Her senses are more alive, her eyes seem to let in more light. Even her body seems lighter.

She needs to stop at her mom's, just north of Lansing, to pick up Murphy and then her trip officially begins.

Twenty minutes later, she pulls up to the white-washed two-story building, a late forties house, with a big front porch. She gulps. She's going to miss 531 Broadway, home of her dreams and games and her childhood. Home of her beloved cherry tree. Just down the road from Mrs. Bender and her fifteen cats. Across the street from her lifelong best friend, Holly. Other than Eli, Holly is still her closest confidante and supporter. But Holly is in Europe right now—a Fulbright Scholarship to some veterinary school.

As soon as the truck is off, both Murphy and her mom burst from the front door. Murphy prances all around the truck joyfully as if looking for someone else. He totally ignores Tessa and she realizes he is looking for Aunt Sadie. Well, that made the most sense. He finally approaches her.

"I know I'm a poor substitute but will you allow me the next dance?" Tessa ruffles his long soft ears. He noses the door of the trailer, so Tessa unlocks the door and the deadbolt. Paul had instructed her to lock both when driving down the road and she promised she always would.

Murphy leaps into the rig. He looks around and sniffs. His tail wags as if he senses something familiar. He hops onto the bed. He lays down for a moment and then jumps off. He runs outside to the truck door and noses the handle. Tessa opens the passenger door and Murphy climbs up over the seat and onto the back cab bed made just for him. He lies down, looking perfectly at home. He jumps right back off and out of the truck to the tailgate and noses that too. Murphy doesn't wait for Tessa to get it all the way open before he jumps up. He sniffs the kayak and looks at her like, "What is this?"

He puts one paw tentatively into the large open kayak, then another, then he gets in and lies down. Briefly. He stands up and, wagging his tail, returns to Tessa.

"I think he knows he's going with you," her mom says.

"Right?"

Her mom has Murphy's day bed and dishes and Murphy watches as they load it in the trailer. Then he noses Tessa's hand. Murphy sits, his eyes solemn.

"Do you know she's not here anymore?" Tessa bends down and hugs him. "Do you know it's just you and me now?"

"Part of me wants to go with you . . ." Her mom is petting Murphy too.

"Mom, I want to do this alone."

"I know, baby. Some of it is selfish and part of it is . . . worry."

"I have Aunt Sadie's shotgun." Tessa grins.

"Oh no."

"Oh yes, I do. Mr. Forsythe insisted."

"But you don't know how to . . ."

"Paul took me to the gun range."

"Paul?"

"The cute garage delivery guy."

"Tessa you haven't done anything with anyone have you?"

"Oh my god, Mom. I'm not going to tell you if I did or

didn't. Wow. You're not like, channeling Jill are you?" Tessa sucks in her breath, immediately regretting her words.

"It's just hard for me to realize you're an adult."

"Everyone else sees it."

"And I promised I wouldn't cry."

Tessa hugs her. "It's only twelve weeks, mom. A school semester is longer. I'll be back the end of July, mid-August the latest. And we'll talk every Wednesday. We can FaceTime. It was cool of Mr. Forsythe to give you Aunt Sadie's iPad."

For a creepy dude, he was thoughtful.

"Come in and have some food before you go." Her mom puts her hand on Tessa's shoulder and turns her toward their home.

Impatient to start, Tessa wants nothing more than to be on the road right now, but what's another hour with her mom in the scheme of things?

BETH WATCHES HER only daughter leave. She tries not to cry. She puts on a brave face and hates her relatives for forcing this issue. Damn them and their greed. This one pure soul, who wouldn't hurt anyone if she could help it, sent out, alone, on a task any of them could have done easily.

She knows their whispers, how her daughter has taken a leave from school, how Beth works two jobs while this girl fritters away her time. Beth remembers being nineteen. She remembers the angst of learning about her body, about college, about Gabe.

Her first meeting with Gabe had been so innocuous. She had been lying on the sheet she dragged everywhere so she could flop it on the ground and study in the sunshine. So she could flop it in someone's living room and be at home. Wherever this sheet was and she on top of it, she was at home. It was her place in the world, this sheet.

She and her sheet were in the middle of the gardens at the university and someone blocked out the sun for the briefest second.

His smiling eyes, the curly topped hair, and his infectious gap-toothed grin caught her immediately.

"Mind if I sit?" he asked. "You know, I see you all over campus, and you never sit in a regular chair unless the teacher asks you to. Why is that?"

"I like to be grounded." She laughed. "This blanket grounds me. I like being down here, next to the earth, my feet bare, the scent of the earth rising up to me."

Gabe smiled. "My mom always called me a little heathen, because I'm the same way. I like being on the ground, or outdoors."

It was that moment that Gabe caught her heart. There was no Mark, or any of the other boys she'd been dating. Within three months they married.

Beth finished Occupational Therapy school. Gabe finished his wildlife degree, but jobs were at a premium, so he worked construction, till something in his field opened.

But then, Beth was pregnant, and construction was paying more than any seasonal wildlife job.

When the twins were born, Beth insisted she wanted Mark as the godfather. Gabe agreed.

As the twins grew, Gabe noticed T was the most athletic. The most agile, the one most willing to climb a tree. Gabe couldn't wait to take them hunting and fishing. To show them all he knew about the woods.

He was always in the leaves with them, tussling and shouting. Beth watched from her blanket as she read and heard their shouts of glee, and laughter and love.

Tessa always rose early, practically leaping out of bed every morning. As soon as there was a hint of sun it was as if every cell in her body expanded and inhaled and wanted to greedily drink in more daylight. Even in winter, Tessa was always the first awake. Her mom found her downstairs under the kitchen table, doodling on paper, little figures, dreams she was drawing "from memory," she said.

She didn't want food, she didn't want breakfast, she just wanted more paper and crayons and chalks and pencils and paints. Later, in school, she discovered ink and specialized pens. While everyone else was enamored with game boys, phones, and laptops, Tessa was in the back drawing.

At first, the idea of school seemed fine. Her mom told her she'd be able to draw all day. It was not exactly true, but her first week of kindergarten, they did draw a lot. The school was practically kitty-corner to their house.

Her mom had walked her and Eli there the first two days. She showed them how to cross with the light at the busy corner. First straight down from their house. Wait for the light. Even when it was green look both ways because sometimes cars sped through lights. Then wait at the corner and turn left. Repeat.

This day, Eli stayed home with an upset tummy. Tessa had no idea that their mom watched every morning, just to be sure they were safe. At the first corner, by the boarding house, Tessa noticed the knot of kids on the side of the school.

She resisted the urge to dash kitty-corner across the street and join in the fun. Bigger kids were throwing rocks. She was good at throwing rocks and she was anxious to show the big kids how good she was. She swung her lunchbox back and forth impatiently, the light finally turned green. She sprinted across the street and then remembered about speeding cars. Everyone stopped for her and she ran. The next light seemed even slower and she was afraid the school bell would ring before she could join the big group of kids.

Finally, she was on school grounds and raced over to see the excitement. Kids were dashing around finding rocks, and she scooped one up on her way. She pushed her way through the bigger kids, she couldn't wait to show what a good shooter she was and then she saw the black-and-white cat cowering against the brick wall of the school as one of the older kids flung a stone, finding its mark. She dropped her lunchbox and the rock and hovered over the cat.

"Hey! Are you crazy?" a fourth grader shouted at her and tried to pull her away. He couldn't budge her.

"Get out of here. We're gonna hit you instead if you don't move."

"Yeah! Move!" another big kid said and his rock stung her on the base of her head right by her neck. She didn't even flinch.

"No!" she shouted, loud and clear. "You're not hurting this cat anymore."

"It's not your cat. Get away from it. It's a mangy stray."

She didn't obey. She blocked out their shouting and the pelting rocks. More rocks and stones hit her, but the bell rang.

"Oh, let's go," the older ones said.

"The bell rang. Haw! You're going to be late protecting some dumb ass cat!" they called to her.

She didn't move until every last one was in the school. Then she scooped up the cat and took it home. She told her mom everything. Her mom walked back with her to the school and talked with the teacher. Tessa never got in trouble. And Bandi became her cat.

Bandi loved her. She followed her everywhere. She lay on Tessa at night and purred. Tessa felt Bandi's purr go straight into her heart. It was the most delicious feeling in the world.

She began hating school. She was the child with her nose pressed up against the window, wanting to be outside. She was the child who only breathed fully when she was outdoors, running, playing, climbing.

She recreated movies and worlds and played funny games, getting others to join her in her play acting at recess.

One time they crossed an invisible line, where all the boys played. The older boys picked her up and threw her back over the invisible line. They had all the soccer balls. And basketballs. They wouldn't share. The older girls laughed at her and asked, "Why do you want to get all dirty anyway?"

The younger boys in her grade saw what had happened and decide to form a "we don't stop for nobody line" on the girls' side. Even Eli joined this line.

Tessa gathered five or six other little girls and formed a V, like the geese did in the fall. They ran straight for the line of eight or ten boys, with Tessa at the front. Once she got to the line, where the boys had locked arms, she kicked Eli's ankle and slammed a fist in his best friend's ear. The boys howled and ran back to the boy's side. All the older girls and boys were laughing at the young boys.

"Don't make it worse!" a big boy shouted at the crying boys. "Leave them alone. Don't you know women are like hornets and they won't stop?"

Tessa high fived with the other little girls and everyone left them alone from then on. The older boy even threw them a soccer ball every recess, out of respect or to keep them calm, Tessa wasn't really sure and didn't care.

Eli would sleep till ten or eleven, but Tessa had lived half a day by then. She became Gabe's little pet and followed him around everywhere. She stayed up late, reluctant to let Morpheus take her to sleep. In winter, even in the worst of storms, she'd want to be outside, but her mom coaxed her in with hot cocoa made the Anishinaabe way Grandma made it, a lot of cream, a little maple syrup, and a hint of cinnamon.

She watched the different flakes swirl and marry each other and watched the brave birds all puffed up against the wind, their feathers blown around as a gust hit them while they ate thistle and suet and seed.

"Mom, if we're so poor why do you feed the birds?"

"I don't know, Tessa. I just do. We have bird birthmarks. We're meant to take care of the birds."

"And they take care of us?"

"Yes, and they take care of us."

Eli was always shorter, always chubbier, a little slower until they became teenagers, and then he sprouted.

Their dad had an accident. He fell out of his tree stand while hunting. His moods became a little darker and when T insisted on wearing pink and staying indoors closer to her mother, their dad rebelled.

Their mom and dad fought a lot. They visited the grandparents, the day of the bear on the footpath. After that, their parents lived separately. It was when their mom moved them to 531 Broadway. Once a month, Eli and Tessa dutifully visited their father up north.

They usually helped him with outdoor things, gathering firewood, setting traps. Their father belittled Eli because he was chunkier, and slower. Tessa matched Eli, so they went the same pace. But her father knew.

All her young life, T defended Eli, but when they turned sixteen, everything changed. Everything changed that one horrible day in the woods.

CHAPTER 5

JOSH WAITS LIKE a rock. Not a muscle moves. It is six a.m. in Fishtown in mid-May and the charter boys have left. It's unlike Tessa to be late. Josh stays in a crouch, watching various morning delivery folks come and go, and then he sees her familiar pink Adidas jogging down the side street, a graceful black dog running beside her. She's tied her long brown hair back with a pink band and she has a pink backpack on.

He meets her at the sandwich shop next to Carlson's. Standing a foot taller than her, he hugs her and touches foreheads. Murphy wags his tail and lets Josh pet him. Without a word, they turn and head toward the center of the marina docks. They arrive at the fishing vessel and Murphy leaps in as if he's been doing it all his life. Josh cracks a smile. He holds out his hand for Tessa to take and helps her into the boat. He waves to them to settle and throws off the lines from their moorings. Once inside, he does a soft prime and turns the key. The twin mercs rumble to life.

He gently backs out of the slip and throttles forward, wheeling the craft around the other slips and into the channel behind the breakwater wall. Once clear of the wall, he powers forward a bit more, the sun, just edging into Leland, hits Lake Michigan full on. It's flat this morning and Josh raises his speed up a notch. He flips on his radar only once out of the harbor. Josh and the other seasoned operators always spied rookie owners who kept their radar going once in the marina. Depth finding carp or what? Yessirree, Bob, a multimillion dollar yacht and a several thousand-dollar computer system operated by a two-bit captain.

Josh hits eighteen miles an hour, with the smooth water the vessel skims over the deeper, often treacherous undercurrents of this inland sea. Many a ship has been lost in the Manitou Passage and many lives. Sailors from all over the world scoff at this inland sea, only to be taken by it. Josh has total reverence for any water he's on.

Warm and inviting like now, or turn on you in an instant, the weather particular to the Great Lakes can conjure a thundering unseen squall and rush in, creating waves forty feet high. So much more treacherous than the long rollers in the oceans, when cold weather meets warm air over the water, the turbulence can be sudden and frightful. This water, in particular the Manitou Passage, is confined by deep turrets of channels, and several sets of shallow unseen shoals, a bathtub rocking and rolling unpredictably.

Terns skip alongside them, but Josh isn't casting nets today.

Murphy lies at Tessa's feet and Josh smiles again. Texting her the night before, Josh recommended she bring good drinking water, a towel, and a change of clothes. Since they're heading to the Crescent Side, they should be free of prying eyes.

With a recent self-made National Park System budget crisis, some park had overpaid a concessionaire somewhere, there's no official park personnel presence on either South or North Manitou, and there won't be any for another two weeks.

Tessa is totally safe.

Josh made sure of that.

Halfway around the north side, Josh nudges Tessa's foot and gestures to the high sandstone cliffs. There, etched by the west wind are two perfectly conical shapes jutting out from the formation.

"It's Madonna!" Tessa shouts gleefully, clapping her hands.

Josh nods and points upwards. A pair of eagles are soaring

on the morning thermals. He rounds the Wisconsin side of the island, where the old shay train grade can still be easily seen. He knows the slope well—they're closing in on the remnants of the old Crescent Dock.

After a few moments, he cuts the engines and picks along till he finds the outermost post and slowly follows the diagonal line to shore. Later in the season, the lake will lose some depth and the pilings will become visible above the water, but for now, Josh carefully edges his way along. Without a word, Tessa begins disrobing to her suit. She slings on a pair of quick-drying shorts and shimmies to the front of the boat, waiting for Josh's signal.

Josh cuts the engines entirely and lets the momentum and the water propel the vessel forward. He looks out the side, not trusting the depth finder and when he judges that Tessa won't get totally dunked, he nods. He watches her leap fearlessly off the front.

She grabs the bow lines, then guides the craft gently ashore. Murphy leaps off and follows her.

Josh tosses the stern line, and Tessa wraps it just the way he showed her years ago. He throws anchors fore and aft. He believes in being safe. He won't leave the vessel for long. But he believes in thoroughness in all things.

They walk up the dune and spy the one structure still left on this side of the island. A huge old barn.

"That's where AJ White lost his arm in 1912." Josh points to a meadow with a slight depression in it. "Used to be a saw mill. That depression? A pond. The shay train came down the grade over there." He points to the ridge they'd just climbed over. "I'm going back down. No one's around. That depression is the one your Aunt Sadie meant."

"You're not staying and doing ceremony with me?"

"This is for you to do. We've done ceremony before." He

gives her an eagle feather he'd found on one of his earlier trips to the island. He takes an herb from his pocket, wrapped with ribbon. "This is rosemary from the mainland."

"I brought sage too."

He smiles and walks away.

She'll be fine. He knows she doesn't remember the ceremony from when her guts popped out. She would remember that when the time was right.

A STRANGE BACKPACK is propped up against the camper. Tessa is still sitting in the truck staring at it, counting to four when she hears, "Yo! Cuz!" and Joe lopes gracefully over from another campsite.

He leans in on the driver's side with his most charismatic smile.

"I got a leave from nursing school. I can go with you the whole way. Won't that be awesome?"

"Uhm, gee, Joe, I was kind of looking forward to the alone time. You probably should have talked with me first." Tessa opens the door and Joe looks hurt.

"I thought you'd be thrilled. We can share the driving time . . ."

Murphy stays on Tessa's left side away from Joe. A young woman with dreadlocks and big round glasses walks up between the cedars separating the two campsites, smiling, all her beautiful white teeth showing.

"This is Marissa." Joe slings an arm over the girl holding out her hand toward Tessa. Tessa shakes it.

"Cool ride." Marissa looks at the rig. "Mind if I look inside?"

Why yes, I do.

Murphy lies down with a *harummph* by Tessa's camp chair.

"Beautiful dog."

"He doesn't like being petted," Joe says.

"Ahhhh." Marissa nods.

Tessa opens up the rig. "Have a look."

Both Joe and Marissa pop in and the camper sags under Joe's sheer presence.

Yeah, I feel that way too, camper.

"Wow, it's tinier once you're inside, isn't it?" Joe turns from the doorway.

"That's real gold on that vase, isn't it?" Marissa says of the urn.

"Yeah, that's real gold," Tessa says, remaining outside, unpacking the groceries from Leland.

She really doesn't want Joe anywhere around when she visits Eli.

"Marissa's gotta take off tomorrow. She just gave me a ride up here."

She can give you a ride back.

The voice inside Tessa's head is being very forceful. It's all Tessa can do to not let it just pop out of her mouth. She needs more information though. She needs to know why Joe is really here and why he is being so insistent.

"Well, you two have things to talk about." Marissa, seems to pick up on Tessa's vibe. "I'm gonna get some dinner going. Maybe you'd like to join us?" she asks as they leave the camper.

"Maybe," Tessa says. She has the distinct feeling Marissa has cased the place. The carefully placed vacuous look, like, *I really didn't see anything*.

"Where have you been? I got up here at ten this morning, figured I'd catch ya before you took off for the day."

"I had things to do."

"Ahh, the ashes, right? Smart not to take the whole urn with ya. How does that work anyway? You gotta take a picture of where you're at and then send them to old man Forsythe, just so he knows you did it right or something?"

"Pretty much." How the hell does Joe know so much about the procedure? "Look, Joe, this is not going to work. I like ya and everything, but it's a bad move. I want my privacy." Tessa stows the dry goods in a storage container on the outside of the camper, she begins taking the fresh foods inside.

"C'mon, cuz. My dad didn't give me much choice. He says you need a bodyguard. I'll stay out of the way. You do your thing, I'll do mine. I can sleep in the back of the truck."

"Your dad? Tell him I have the shotgun."

Joe's mouth opens and closes. Tessa can't tell if he looks more like a fish or a marionette.

"Wow. He wanted that shotgun real bad." Joe kicks some soft dirt around his toes, looking down at the ground.

"Yeah, he can talk to Forsythe about it." Tessa shakes her head. "In fact, it's his after the trip. I don't give a shit." She returns outside. "You can't come. That's it. Go back to school." She tries to maintain her calm as she carefully folds the brown paper grocery bags.

"Hey, I get this is a touchy situation, given . . . everything."

"Everything what? Just say it." Her patience gone, Tessa turns and faces Joe squarely. He shifts away and looks at the nearby cedar.

"C'mon, why are you being so difficult? You're acting just like a . . ."

"Just like a what? I'm not one of your bitches."

"Wow. This strikes a nerve doesn't it?" He looks her over.

"What the fuck? Why does everyone think I'm so helpless? If y'all thought that, then maybe somebody else should be doing this, but no, you're all too busy. Then you just show . . . How would you like it, roles reversed?"

"Uh, not very well. You'd be cramping my style."

"Exactly."

"Look." Joe drops to the ground, cross-legged style, holding a joint. "I don't have a choice. If I don't go with you, Dad's cutting off the money for nursing school."

"Damn, maybe you should work your way through school like everyone else."

"Look, let's just do a hit or two, calm down, and talk about it a little later."

"I'm not changing my mind." Tessa folds her arms.

"Okay, okay, I get it."

"And don't light that shit up here. It's a federal park, they fine you five hundred dollars."

"No shit?"

"No shit. Go out on the public road. Or anywhere else. Not here."

"Hey." Joe gets up as he dusts his shorts off. He sticks the joint in the breast pocket of his flannel shirt. "Thanks for the heads up."

Tessa is so mad, she's not hungry. She decides to pour part of Aunt Sadie into a spice jar. She stows her up with the dried foods above the stove. She stashes the vase and the remaining ashes out of sight. She locks up the camper, then jumps in the truck with Murphy.

She just starts driving. She doesn't know where she is going, but she doesn't want to be anywhere near Joe, or Marissa, or their tent. She contemplates calling Forsythe, but what could he really do? Call Uncle Chuck and have him pull off Cousin Joe? Maybe he could hold something over their heads. Why did Uncle Chuck really want Joe to come along anyway? The fact they know her route creeps her out. She might call Forsythe and change it up a little.

A little south of Empire she finds a road leading to the beach. There are cars there, but to the left is another dirt road.

She drives down it till it ends. It's a Benzie county seasonal road and she gets out with Murphy and starts down a trail that leads west to the water. It takes a long time to wind around the flats and some rises. Josh told her that a long time ago the shores were even further apart. That maybe the ridge on North Manitou had been underwater. That was when the ancients hunted Mastodon, before there was even water, the hills were high and the water came in and flattened everything down. Some of the ridges she is passing by could be ancient burial mounds, and older shorelines.

She hears a flutie bird in the woods and spies enough poison ivy to know that she'd have to rinse Murphy down pretty well before hugging on him too much. At the water Murphy jumps in and paddles around. Tessa throws sticks for him and he doesn't tire. Loons, further out, sing their distinctive yodel song. It's nearing sunset. She takes a picture of the setting sun grazing the water and sends it to Dina. *It's not the same without you.* She looks at the words and deletes the message. *Great way to begin the trip.* She hits send.

An ache in her gut tells her it's time to return. As they cut back through the trails, the dwindling light, the singing solitary flute bird, the trees just beginning to bud leaves, all of it is stirring a memory. It's a vague thought, an uneasy sense, churning.

Churling.

All of a sudden, despite her growling, hungry stomach, she vomits. Murphy looks at her unsurprised as he chews on grass, as if, *Yeah, what else ya got?*

"Wow." Tessa takes a swig of water and rinses her mouth out.

TESSA SITS IN the truck, looking at the camper, bordering somewhere between rage and disgust. A small campfire is dying out at her campsite, and a light is on in the camper, which is now rocking and rolling unceremoniously with fuck sounds coming from it.

Joe and Marissa.

A half-empty Jaeger fifth is propped in the seat of a camp chair.

Are you fucking serious?

Before she knows it, she is at the camper, yanking the door open, and without looking, shouts, "Get the fuck out!"

"Oh shit."

"Now!"

She fumes. Murphy is still in the truck, his head cocked, carefully watching her.

A series of scrambling noises, a giggle, which just infuriates her more, the steps creak under Joe's weight. His flannel shirt is open, showing his muscled chest and flat abs. He's holding something in his hands. Marissa scrambles out behind him, her big lens glasses on, and a throwback hippie shirt over shorts. Neither one of them are wearing anything on their feet. Their feet are filthy from tromping around in the dirt all day.

Oh joy.

"Hey, we were worried about you. You didn't come home for dinner, nothing."

"How the fuck did you get in the camper?"

"You left it open."

"No. Try again."

Joe opens his hand—a set of keys. "Dad used the camper for hunting trips. He still had a set."

Tessa holds out her hand. "Now."

"But Dad will kill me."

Tessa is unmoved. "Look, if this is going to work, it's my rules."

Joe's face changes. "Really?" He drops the keys in her open palm.

"Yeah, send Marissa on her way tomorrow."

"Wow, cuz, that's cool. That's really great. I'm glad you thought it over."

After rinsing Murphy down, and stripping the bed, and wiping the floor of all the dirt footprints, Tessa finally pulls out some cheeses and homemade bread. After a few bites, her head droops, once, twice, and exhausted, she locks the door, pulls a chair over in front of it, and slumps into the unmade bed. Fully clothed, she pulls a blanket over her. Still no text from Dina, but she has twenty from Billy.

THE FOLLOWING NIGHT, after convincing Joe to buy another bottle of Jaeger, Tessa sits at the campfire while he grills steaks. He's got his iPhone playing Bob Marley . . . and he's full of ideas for the trip.

"So I figure when we go up to Pictured Rocks, we can catch up with some old buds of mine from Marquette. That sound cool?"

"Sure."

"That's great, because they have some contacts for going over to Grand Island and stuff. It's too bad we don't have more time, because it would be nice to go to the Porcupine Mountains and do a little hiking, right?"

"Yeah, that would be awesome."

Tessa hands him the Jägermeister. He takes a hefty swing and hands it back to her. She lifts it to her lips.

Joe turns what he calls hobo fries, wrapped in tinfoil over some coals in the fire. He is being totally solicitous, cooking dinner, offering to clean up. He already helped Tessa hook the truck up for their anticipated departure in the morning.

"This is such a perfect night. I think I'll sleep right here by the fire." He smiles.

Tessa smiles back and hands him the Jaeger again. "I'd like to stop at the Cut River on our way. I hear there's some great fishing."

"Dude! How awesome would that be, catch our own dinner? I'm great at cleaning fish."

As the night wears on and dinner turns into dessert, Joe is quite the culinary hero at campfires, he's made a peach cobbler. He's clueless when the rufee hits him.

Yawning, stretching out before the fire, a full tummy and all of the Jaeger gone, Joe's face is upturned toward the stars, his snoring a resounding echo through the campground. Then and only then, does Tessa fire up the cherry bombers, pulls from the site, and leaves Joe behind.

CHAPTER 6

TESSA ROUSES HERSELF early from the roadside park. After a quick jog with Murphy, a cup of piping hot cocoa, and a dash of cheese and bread, she pulls into the parking lot lined with vehicles of varying shapes and sizes, all waiting for the doors to open for visiting day.

Even among the eclectic gathering of cars, trucks, and a few Harleys, Tessa's camper and truck stand out. It's not too long before a handful of men and maybe one or two women glance over.

Tessa slides out and sure as shit three or four guys in muscle shirts and tats meander over and ask if they can look under the hood.

She obliges them and they whistle at how beautiful the engine is and is it a '68?

"They don't make metal like this anymore," one guy with a handlebar moustache says. He is opening and closing the passenger door with a satisfactory whump. When he notices Murphy staring at him from the day bed, he quits.

"Are those cherry bombers on the exhaust?" another asks.

One even drops to the pavement and exclaims, "Not a leak anywhere!"

"Damn! A 4 barrel Holley carb!"

Sighing with visions of the engine dancing in their heads the guys wander off to check in for visitor's day. Tessa could see these guys as if they were ten years old waiting for their first car. Funnier yet is once she's inside waiting for Eli, the tat guys are all macho and business, their huge biceps flexing on their respective tables, impassive as they speak with their relatives, or friends. They don't really acknowledge each other either, as if they hadn't just spoken outside.

When they catch Tessa's eye, they smile and nod and she hears snatches of, "Cherry '68 out in the lot. 390."

"Pristine."

"No rust, nothing. Metal as heavy as shit."

Eli bursts in, hugs her fiercely, then holds her at arm's length and smiles. "The pink is a nice touch."

Their features are identical, the high cheek bones, the dark brown eyes. Tessa is almost looking in a mirror but Eli has a pronounced Adam's apple and he is easily six inches taller than her. That, and he has a moustache.

"You look great."

"So do you."

"Where are you staying?" He motions for them to sit.

"I was at DH Day, but I'm on the road now. How are you, really?"

They hold hands and it isn't strange to Tessa at all.

"I am psyched I'm getting out this year. It could be as soon as three months."

"Seriously? I know Mom said Forsythe hooked her up with a different lawyer for you . . ."

"Yeah. I don't know who Forsythe is, but he's an angel in my book. I have a shark on my side now. They still want to get me for . . ."

"Dad."

He nods. "But no one knows where he went."

Eli is staring straight at the table. In their twin speak energy Tessa knows he's lying. She knows he knows exactly what happened to Dad but a steely part has come down between them and he is unreadable.

Neither speak. Tessa is frozen like in the snow that day. Eli, still staring at the table with their hands clasped even tighter now, whispers, "Don't go back there, Tessa."

"I can't remember any of it."

"Good." Then he looks into her eyes with his own soul back inside him. "Tell me where you've been and where you go next . . ."

AFTER VISITING ELI, Tessa turns the rig toward Ludington. Wisconsin is not in the plans and it's not on the itinerary but she is changing things up fast.

Forsythe finally calls back and she fills him in on the visit from Joe.

"Is it possible to do Lake Superior at the end of the trip instead of now?"

"Yes, by all means. I'll have a talk with your relatives. Make sure that they understand collecting any inheritance will hinge on them letting you proceed unfettered."

Forsythe is pissed, Tessa can hear it in his voice. He might be a creepy dude, but he's showing her he has her back.

"I'd like time to re-think the itinerary because they obviously have a copy of it."

"That's fine, but the route was made for the time of year and the way it made the most sense."

"I'll get as far as Prairie du Chien, Wisconsin in the next couple of days, as long as I hit somewhere on the Mississippi, that will be okay, right?"

"Yes. I trust you implicitly, Tessa. You're doing the right thing. Get back with me on the changeups any time this week. By then I should have the rest of the family on board."

"Thanks, Mr. Forsythe."

As Tessa drives, her memories are triggered by little steeples of rural churches along the road.

The few times they went to church Tessa was so bored she counted bricks on the top of the wall to the right of the altar. If she made it all the way through without Eli interrupting her to play paper, scissors, rock, she began counting all the bricks on the top line to the left of the altar, to make sure they matched up. Sometimes she got down two or three rows before her imagination kicked in.

Her mind settled into some sort of dream world where she became a Pegasus/unicorn and she was above everyone, flying over their heads.

No one ever saw her because they were all staring straight ahead, trying to stay awake too.

Since they didn't see her, she flew to the rafters above the empty church choir section and settled in comfortably until she got bored. Then she flew over everyone's head, recognizing Mr. Knepple's bald head without his hat on, and Mr. Shaggy Hippie Dippie dude, as her mom called him, and smelled stuff that seemed like church incense but was sweeter.

Her mom only took them on festive occasions like Palm Sunday, when they got fronds, or Ash Wednesday when the priest smudged ash on their foreheads with his big fat thumb and then they walked around all day, sanctimonious with their special thumb cross imprint that occasionally dropped ash into their eyes.

Tessa's absolute favorite day was St. Blaze day. The priest crossed two candles at their throats and anointed them so they wouldn't get sore throats, or scarlet fever, or something worse.

As Tessa drives, she hears again Great Aunt Sadie saying she left the Church when the priest spoke one too many times about the woman obeying the husband.

"You mark my words," Aunt Sadie said to all the girls, "you don't let anyone disrespect you. You don't let me do it, you don't let any man do it. You don't let anyone do it, you hear me? Not even the Church. Especially not the Church!"

The further Tessa gets away from Traverse City and her cousin, the easier she's breathing. She checks the time. In a few short hours she'll be on the water again.

ELI VIEWS TESSA as his protector, even though he is bigger and stronger now. Of all the people he needs to spend time with, it's with her first, even though he knows the conversation will be difficult and about their dad.

He can't talk to her now, while he's here in prison. It's impossible. He will not allow her to deal with the truth without him near. He's a part of it too. It's his hate that drive the situation.

When his father took a closed fist and hit Tessa in the head, Eli's animal rage exploded. He had no idea what he was saying or doing and each time his father pushed him off or dared him to try again, Eli grew blind. He lost track of time and they sparred and hit and tumbled and Eli didn't feel any of it, not until his father was choking the life out of him, crushing his windpipe with his forearm, all his weight bearing down on Eli's throat.

Just as he began losing sight, just as he began blacking out, he heard a thud and liquid splattered his face. The relief of the weight being off him almost came too late. He was clenching at his throat with both hands, trying to tear the skin apart, fighting to get his windpipe open, he was still not breathing, but he was on his knees and pulling and pulling until first a half breath, then another, his head on the ground as he kept pleading inside for his throat to open. Finally, miraculously, it did and when he could take in a gulp, he leaned back on his knees and saw two forms lying in the snow.

His dad with part of his scalp and face almost peeled off. A bloody knife still in his right hand. Eli threw up.

"Tessa! Tessa!" His voice sounded foreign and raspy and not his. "Tessa?"

She lay forward in the pile they had mushed down. Face planted in the snow. Eli begged her to be alive, please don't be dead.

She was breathing and when he lifted her and held her he was crying like a child. His breaths were fuller with each sob. When her stomach cramped and she pushed off him, they both look down and saw the ribbon of intestine bulging out.

AFTER PURCHASING HER ferry ticket for the SS Badger, Tessa is in a laundromat, cleaning all the bedding Joe and Marissa used to whack Willy Wonka into Wonderland.

She discovers the storage under the bed holds half-a-dozen large, black binders with dates.

She opens one labelled 1955-1961 and four or five tan old-style composition books tumble out. *1955-1956*, *1959-1961* . . . Tessa picks one up and it opens at the middle to a black-and-white photograph of a really young Great Aunt Sadie and Uncle Percy standing among some sage brush, arms around each other. Her arms are barely over where his butt must be, and he's leaning down a little. They both have dark hair, and Sadie's is curly ringlets and way longer than Tessa remembers ever seeing it.

They look like they're about twenty-one or twenty-five. It's hard to tell. Young.

Tessa reads an entry below it. "After his long hike, Percy returned to camp to find a string of clothes leading into the Pinyon pine. First a sandal, then some shorts, a pair of panties . . ."

She feels her cheeks burning. "Oh my God. This is porn . . ."

The description continues. "He comes upon the vision he so anticipates. A lovely minx, curled up in the blanket and sun, as if she is asleep . . . just for him."

Gulp.

Tessa closes the journal, then she sees a long, thin envelope with her name in an old person's scrawl on it that must have fallen out with the clump of journals.

> Tessa, you've found some travel journals that I was entrusted with among your aunt's possessions. I hand these over somewhat reluctantly, but I trust you will protect the contents herein and be judicious about the details you share. Your aunt specified she thought these journals might be illuminating when spreading the ashes and add some depth to the task at hand.

Oh yeah, they add depth all right, if any of the rest of it is going to be like this.

CHAPTER 7

ONCE SHE BOARDS the ferry with the truck and trailer, Tessa finally breathes fully. She leashes Murphy and puts his service dog jacket on him. Mr. Forsythe had been thorough; he told her there might be places only service dogs were allowed. He'd assured her Murphy was fully trained as a service dog and to use the jacket when necessary.

"If anyone asks, he is trained for high glucose levels for diabetics."

"But I'm not diabetic."

"He has other . . . talents, shall we say? I am very confident his skills will benefit you on this journey."

She climbs the metal stairs from the belly of the SS Badger. Long semis and campers are part of her contingent. Everyone is moving from their vehicles to the upper deck.

Murphy pays little attention to other service dogs or people. They sit outside in the fresh air and people watch. He lies at her feet, his head over her right foot.

Tessa's phone rings, and she's excited to see Dina is FaceTiming her. "Where are you now, you little imp?"

"I'm on the water. You can't tell anyone. I'm going to Wisconsin."

"That's not on your itinerary."

"I had a messed up visit from Cousin Joe."

"Oh shit. No! Really?"

"Really."

Dina looks awesome. She's lying on her bed, her long hair disheveled, her head resting in one hand as she holds the phone and speaks.

Tessa is hopelessly in love. "I miss you."

"I miss you too, punkin."

"I didn't think I would."

"It's only been, what? Three days? Four?"

Tessa sighs. "Yeah, I know . . ."

The ship's horn blasts.

"Wow that's loud! Even over the phone."

Murphy's up on all fours, looking around nervously. Tessa pets him and cuddles him so Dina can see.

"Oh, poor Murph," Dina coos. "He's like, the coolest dog. What a great jacket. You oughta take pics everywhere you go and post 'em. Murph and me on the high seas."

"I would if my uncle wasn't being such a prick."

"Uh-oh."

"Yeah. Dickhead. Sending Joe after me. I don't trust any of them. Neither does Murph. He won't even let Joe pet him."

"Good judge of character." Dina laughs.

"I'll just learn how to make a little montage, or movie or something. Will have to show you when you come to Canada with me."

"I'll *try* to come to Canada with you. I still don't have the okay from my job or anything."

Tessa wonders what the anything is. Xander? But she refrains from asking.

As the ferry pulls underway, the wind blows Tessa's hair into her face, so she shifts to the side and sees a really cute, older woman in a white uniform, with blue-and-gold shoulder caps, watching her and Murphy. The woman grins when their eyes meet. She winks and moves on through the crowd, asking folks how they are? Everyone settling in?

"Who are you looking at?" Dina is smiling.

"How did you know?" Tessa points the phone at the uniformed woman. She hasn't learned how to reverse the picture yet. She knows there is a way. She aims the phone back at herself.

"Oh yeah, if you're into old ladies."

"She's not that old." Tessa laughs.

"A woman in uniform is handsome, I'll give you that."

"She winked at me."

"Oooh, I'm gonna be jealous."

Tessa smiles broadly.

"God, you're beautiful." Dina looks at her with that open love look. "I promise. I will do my best to meet up with you in Canada."

"You better."

"Okay, hon, it's the waitress job for me. Kisses. Keep sending pics. I love it."

"K." Tessa hesitates. "Love you!"

"Love you too."

A message had popped in while they were talking. Billy.

Can we FaceTime now?

Lord. She's going to have to let him down.

Bad signal.

She shuts the phone off. She stows it in her backpack. Just as she reaches for a bottle of water, a shadow crosses in front of her. The woman in uniform is standing there, petting Murphy.

"Love your dog."

"Murphy."

"Well, hi, Murphy, nice to meet you." Murphy is wagging his tail and the woman reaches in her pocket.

"I think I have something for you." She looks at Tessa to see if it's okay.

Tessa nods. She wishes she could control the flushing she feels rushing to her cheeks. Up close the woman is even more striking, with her curly topped hair and trim figure. Murphy salivates as he senses the biscuit, drool hitting the deck before he gobbles it from the woman's open palm.

"Hey." Tessa laughs. "That's not nice. Be gentle, Murphy."

"Oh, not many can resist my homemade treats." The woman's eyes are a greenish brown and the smile reaches all the way up to her crinkles. "I'm first mate Schwab. Schwabbie to my friends."

Tessa stands and shakes her hand. "Tessa."

"First time on the SS Badger?"

"First time on a ferry."

"If you have any concerns at all, please find me." She rubs Murphy's head again. "I'll be back."

Only when the first mate moves away, does Tessa see that more than a few people noticed their exchange. A couple with a young son, waiting to meet First Mate Schwab, follow after her.

An older couple trail after them.

A woman, sitting on the bench across from Tessa, smiles. She has to be at least seventy years old. "She sure took a shine to you."

"I think it was my dog." Tessa feels herself blush again. People walk between them, so the old woman stands unsteadily and treads carefully to her, her hands out from her sides a little. She is quite tall.

"Still getting my sea legs."

Murphy's head is instantly in the woman's lap as she sits.

"Oh, my." The woman's white pants now have doggie drool on them.

"I'm so sorry!"

"Oh, don't worry. I just lost my Jasper, so this is good. He must smell him on me. What's your dog's name?" The woman is whispering to him, her face down by his.

Tessa is astonished. Murphy never lets anyone put their face close to him, except for Tessa.

"Murphy."

"He's so soft." The woman continues petting Murphy while looking at Tessa.

"Traveling far?"

"A little bit," Tessa admits. "I have a camper down below."

"Oh! So do I. I think I live more on the road than I do off it these days."

"Do you like it?"

"Oh, yes. I never tire of traveling. I have lots of friends all over the US and Canada. I quit going to Mexico when they started targeting the AARP crowd." The woman grins. "I'm sorry. My name is Madeline Sweet. Maddy for short."

They shake hands.

"Tessa Williams. It's kind of pricey isn't it? The ferry ride."

"Yes, but it saves so much on driving, and gas. These sorts of shortcuts I don't mind. Are you on vacation?"

"Sort of." Tessa doesn't want to go into detail. "It's sort of a family thing."

"Very nice."

"You both have campers?" A man next to Madeline pokes his head around. His eyes are magnified behind his glasses. He wears a tan cowboy hat that seems to dwarf him. He has a nice smile and handsome moustache. A woman in glasses with curly long hair leans over from beside him and waves. She's too far out of hearing.

"Chris," he points to himself, "and Cindy. We're the Hoopers. We travel all over the US and Canada in our fifth wheel."

Madeline seems to know what that is and proceeds to ask Chris all about it. In the course of about three minutes they've exchanged details like who's going where and what's on their agenda. All Tessa gets out of it is one's going north and the other is going south and they're both heading west eventually. Then she notices Chris is in a small electric wheelchair.

"We're all road hoboes," he says.

"That's a nice hat." Madeline gestures.

"It's a Stetson." He offers it for Madeline to try.

"You look good in it." He grins. "Better than me."

Madeline turns to Tessa and she nods in agreement.

"Hats are wasted on me." Madeline laughs and offers it to Tessa who shakes her head no.

"We're going to case the place inside, if you two care to join us." Chris winks and expertly wheels his ride through the constant weaving of crowd before and aft the ship.

"Coming?"

Tessa nods. "In a bit. I'd like to stay outside for a while. Nice meeting you." She shakes Madeline's hand and only then realizes how strong she is. For not being super large, Madeline's hands are blocky and worker like.

"Nice meeting you. See you down the road."

EVEN THOUGH IT'S dark when the vehicles disembark the Badger, Tessa is wide awake and decides to make miles. The Hoopers and Madeline are hitting a county campground nearby, but eager to see the Mississippi, Tessa elects to drive further.

She makes it as far as Kettle Moraine State Forest. Since it's still spring and kids are in school, she finds her pick of places in an all but deserted campground. One or two sites occupied, Tessa moves as far away as she can from neighbors and noses into a site that promises a lakeside view in the morning.

It's already Wednesday. Time for the Mommy Call. Tessa knows that's probably not a nice way to refer to it, but it's not meant to be derogatory. It just is. She and Murphy finish running around the quiet campground and down to the doggie swim area bordering Ottawa Lake.

He's under the picnic table, licking his fur softly. She has a cup of warm cocoa and takes a deep breath. Eight a.m. Wisconsin time, nine a.m. Michigan. Mom doesn't go to work till ten.

Her mom picks up as if she's been sitting on the iPad.

"Oh my God, I can see you. Oh, it looks beautiful there."

"Hi, Mom, everything's good. Great even."

"It is? No flats or anything?"

"No. Nothing."

"No bad characters?"

Sure, if you want to count the relatives.

"Smooth sailing."

"How's Murphy?"

Tessa moves the phone below the picnic table, cocky enough to hit the reverse photo button.

"Oh that's a neat trick. I thought you were going to show me your belly button."

"Funny."

Tessa brings the phone back to her. Her mom's eyes are bagged up, like she hasn't been sleeping, and they have the dark circle raccoon look.

"Mom. You need more iron. And more sleep. Maybe you'd better eat some liver and onions."

"Ewww. You're right about the iron though. Oh my, this iPad rats me out."

"Your hair looks nice," Tessa offers.

Her mom is playing with the screen.

"What are you doing?"

"Oh, Mr. Forsythe told me if I put my finger on my own picture I could move it around. He's right. There, now I can see you better."

"You're gonna become a techno junkie."

"I've been playing with it. Did you know there's a

crocheting chat group online? You can even all sit around and crochet together, but most of the time it's like a support group, I swear."

Tessa shakes her head. "And you're worried about me and bad characters? Some of those chat crotchetier could be Farley and his other brother Farley, waiting to meet up with you at a Java Juice and take you for a shrimp ride."

"We can hear each other's voices if not see each other. Unless they have really high voices I don't believe any Farleys are going to find me. Let's get back to you. Did you see Eli?"

"I did, and he's excited about the new lawyer."

"Won't that be wonderful if he is out once you're back?"

Tessa nods.

"Who else have you heard from?"

"Billy."

"Is that all?"

Tessa hesitates. "Dina."

"You're enamored with her, aren't you?"

No! I'm fucking in love with her.

Tessa lets out a lot of wind as she sighs this time.

"Oh, I know what that means."

"What's what mean?"

"That gassy sound you make, like a balloon losing all its air at once."

"That's so not funny, Mom. Is that what these little Wednesday chats are going to be like? Because not enough states let me drink in them to do this for the entire time."

"I just don't want you to get hurt."

"Dina's not going to hurt me. She's busy. She has jobs, and school and . . ."

"Xander."

"Exactly."

Even her mom is attracted to Xander. All the older ladies are. He can charm the pants off most anyone. Except Tessa. And he's tried. Tessa told Dina who just laughed it off with, "If he hadn't tried with you, I'd worry he was sick."

"So once you're past Indiana which road do you take, 65? Or 75 to Florida?"

Her mother has said a whole paragraph and Tessa has to catch up with her.

"Uh, I dunno." She realizes she's twisting the hair by her ear. She drops her hand. "Sorry."

"Oh, I know, it's boring talking to your mother, but will you do me a favor?"

"Maybe."

"Will you call me tonight? I have to get ready for work."

"There's not much to tell."

"I know, honey. I just want to hear your voice. I'll keep it short. Let's try for eight, okay?"

Tessa nods because she can't seem to find it in her right now to say no.

CHAPTER 8

IN PRAIRIE DU CHIEN, Wisconsin the Mississippi is wide and slow. Tessa stands on the banks as she contemplates where to spread ashes.

"Are you kayaking the river?" a voice behind her asks.

She turns to see a young man, about her height, a bit robust, hair on his chest, in kayak shorts and shoes, finely muscled legs, carrying a single kayak over his shoulders.

"Uhm, I've never actually kayaked a river. I wouldn't know how to get back." Tessa points to the truck and camper.

"Nice rig." He looks her over as if making a decision. "I already posted my car downstream and rode my bike back." He indicates a bike locked up at the park. "You could just leave your rig at the Villa Louis Museum and tell them we're kayaking downstream and will be back this afternoon." He sticks his hand out. "My name is J Prince. Not like the singer. I just don't like my first name, so call me Jay or Prince."

"Tessa."

Murphy lets Prince pet him.

"Okay," Tessa agrees. "But I've only kayaked a lake. Not a river."

"Well, the Mississippi is basically a lake at this point. A series of large basins divided by the locks and dams."

Tessa has no clue what Prince is talking about, but she nods along.

Once the museum folks, who know Prince, okay Tessa leaving her rig, Prince carries her kayak for her down to the river. He stands in the cool waters of the Mississippi, holding the bow, and Murphy readily jumps in and lies down, then Tessa steps in the middle, like Paul had shown her.

She sits and Prince hands her the paddle and shoves her out. She drifts toward midstream, panic rising in her, but he quickly joins her.

"Let's just float a little," Prince suggests. "Let the river carry us."

As they float, Tessa's fast beating heart returns to normal. They talk about nothing and everything. Pretty soon they are casually paddling, and then they are really moving downstream.

"This is fun!" Tessa exclaims. "And easy. Easier than in the lake."

"That's because the river is helping you." Prince smiles, then points his paddle up. "Look there." A giant thunderbird is painted onto the limestone cliffs.

"Is that real?" Tessa asks.

"Mmmm, not really. Some hippies in the seventies painted it. That's what my folks say. Then every year some historical group keeps up on it, near where the original was."

"But how do they get there?"

"These days they rappel, and use harnesses, maybe? I don't really know."

"So why are you kayaking?"

"I'm training for a triathlon, but it's still too cold to swim, so I run and bike and kayak."

"You're ambitious."

"I just like to be outside." Prince smiles. "What's your story?"

Tessa pulls out a little zip lock bag of ashes.

"Great Aunt Sadie. Took a trip with Uncle Percy around the states and now I'm spreading her for the family."

"Are you serious? That's sort of awesome."

"Yeah, actually I have to do ceremony."

Prince looks at her blankly.

"It's a family thing."

"That's cool, but you might want to wait till we get down to the Piasa bird."

"What's that?"

"It's another painted bird on the limestone. The big one is further down the river in Alton. That one has a lot of imitators. The original was mined out a long time ago, so they put one down by Alton, and there's one up here. Some locals insist the Piasa belongs up here anyway. And, it's really not supposed to be a bird. It's supposed to be supernatural dwarves; little people with super powers."

"Like aliens?"

Prince chuckles. "Yeah, maybe."

"Well, I'd better not tell Mom. She's into that stuff. She'd be here in a heartbeat. Great Aunt Sadie was little and she definitely had power," Tessa muses as they paddled away from the thunderbird.

And definitely revered.

"When we break for lunch we should be close. There's a nice wide sandy beach there too. Do you need fire for your ceremony?"

Tessa shakes her head. "I have a candle and a feather and some sage."

After lunch, out of respect, Prince stays back as Tessa walks the beach and looks at the painted creature. Prince said the one in Alton had wings, but this one looks more like a dragon, with a tail flipped around almost to its head.

Its eyes are shiny and its mouth is open. It reminds Tessa of Maori warriors in New Zealand. Prince is right. This is the perfect place.

Tessa closes her eyes and gets real quiet. Murphy sits beside her. She calls in her guides and all the people that have gone before her. She calls in the four directions. Most of this she does silently, then she calls in the elements. Sometimes she'll find a feather on the way, or a rock, like a heart-shape rock or quartz. Today she is just with Murphy and Prince, so she uses Josh's feather. She lights the sage and cleanses herself with it, and Murphy. And the ashes. Then she walks into the water and blesses her Great Aunt once more, and releases the ashes. Then she takes a picture of the ashes and the water as she has every time. And sends it in a message to Mr. Forsythe.

"I didn't know iPhones were part of ceremony," Prince calls out.

Tessa grins and walks toward him. "Ahhh yes, the sacred iPhone family ceremony."

"That's pretty cool. I respect you for taking the time to care for your Aunt that way."

"I'm doing it for Aunt Sadie *and* the family."

"Murphy seems to take it pretty seriously too."

"He does, doesn't he?"

Prince points to the purple bird foot birthmark on her left thigh. "That's a cool mark."

"Yeah, my twin has one just like it." Tessa wishes she hadn't said that.

"Well, why isn't your twin here?"

"He's got a job. Couldn't take time off." Tessa hates lying so she wills herself to believe it's true, in a way.

Prince doesn't dwell on it. "Let's scoot. We have a few miles to cover yet."

CHAPTER 9

WHEN JOSH FIRST found Tessa and Eli, he saw Eli crying and trying to hold Tessa's intestines in. Josh snapped his knife in the bloodied snow and commenced to treat her like he would any animal on the farm; a cow with a prolapsed uterus, a calf with fescue and half a hoof gone. He opened his kit and, thankful that Tessa had passed out, proceeded to field stitch her.

He ordered Eli to grab the travois in the back of the truck so Eli could trek Tessa out. He did not want to chance the jumbling of the truck with his fragile stitching. They bundled her tightly in a blanket wrap so as Eli pulled the travois, she wouldn't be jostled. And he directed Eli to the shorter route, only five hundred feet to where an ambulance siren was already approaching.

"Go! Now. Meet them over the hill. Straight to Traverse City. Tell them she fell on her knife."

He handed Eli his.

"Now!" Eli, still in shock, nodded dumbly as he gazed at the other figure in the snow.

"I'll take care of everything else. The less you know, the better. Go!"

Josh knelt next to Gabe and turned him over. Grimacing, he gently lifted the part of the scalp that had been almost cut clean through. He wrapped tight the head wound before heaving Gabe's lifeless body over his shoulder.

Josh carried him over the snow that would melt first in the next day or two with the rains and forty degree temperatures. He walked right in their footprints they had made coming up the hill. He belted the body in his truck and trussed him up. He took a moving blanket from the bed of the truck and wrapped Gabe in it. He put sunglasses and an oversized wool hat on him. Gabe looked as if he was sleeping.

Josh drove out, bucking and spinning the way he came in. He would return to this spot at dawn and, with any luck, no one would be the wiser till then.

Josh kayaked with the lifeless form across the river. His strokes were methodical and consistent. The body in front sat hunched over, unmoving. Almost frozen.

Josh's cousins were waiting for them on the Canadian side. The fog was barely lifting in the early morning hours. Josh tried to keep his mind on the task at hand and not worry about Tessa. She was in good hands now. She was strong and he had to trust she would survive.

The cousins pulled the kayak in. They helped Josh move the limp form from the front and treat his body carefully, like an elder, like glass.

They made a strange contingent of men with long hair in Levi jackets and jeans, muddied work boots, a small parade in the thicket of swamp cedars. Silently they walked, carrying a gurney. Two Ford trucks waited for them, indistinguishable from all the other logging work trucks and crew cabs in that part of Ontario. Chainsaws, fuel cans, bar oil. They rumbled down the two track and eventually to a deserted hard-top road.

No cars for miles. The lead truck turned right and a hand waved. The truck the elder's body was in turned left and began its journey. First to Sudbury, and a small shack a mile off the train tracks and eventually to the original clan; the caribou followers.

Josh was already halfway across the river with one final task to finish. After stowing the kayak on the ladder rails of his truck, Josh drove the three hours back. This time he came in from the east on the Rayle Road. Just as he thought, half the snow had melted in the several hours he had been away. He parked, found a barely discernable path, and hiked to a deer blind left over from the fall. Gabe's deer blind.

He climbed the stand and waited. As the sun rose higher and higher, he believed his relatives had deserted him. Then he heard a crack. A step. Another step. Turkey?

Josh dared not move. He waited. The young doe came in. He steeled his heart. He couldn't feel right now. He slowly moved the crossbow to sight. Her nose twitched. But she was here. For him. For Tessa. For Eli. Yes, even for Gabriel. He pressed the release. Just behind her right shoulder. She stumbled and went down.

Josh was on the ground and over her. His breath fogged over her neck as he held her and slit her throat. She bled out and still he did not allow himself any emotion. He placed the plastic over his shoulders and carried her over his back, forelegs in his right hand, and back legs in his left. And he placed her over the blood pile from yesterday.

He field dressed her here, from neck to anus, and was thankful she was too young to be carrying fawn. He prayed over her, he called her and asked for forgiveness. And smeared her blood over Tessa's blood and Gabriel's blood and he prayed that this was enough to keep everyone safe.

Then he carried her again to his truck and covered her with the same moving blanket from the day before.

Once he was on the road toward Peshawbestown, then and only then did he let himself cry.

CHAPTER 10

TESSA WORRIES HOW she will make up Lake Superior, The St. Lawrence Seaway, and Bay of Fundy, way north and east. Would she do it at the end of her trip? All she knows now is she is heading to Stone Mountain Georgia and then on to Florida and the Keys.

She's listening to iTunes with her ear buds. But as she flips her visor down to block the rising eastern sun, she sees a variety of CDs in a flap.

She pulls one out. It's unmarked save for "Good Driving Music" printed neatly from something like a Sharpie.

She pops it in and is instantly greeted with blaring lyrics from "Kryptonite."

Tessa fumbles for volume, eject, anything. She ends up jumping a track to Bon Jovi's, "It's My Life."

"Lord. Auntie. Scare me 'bout half to death." It's quite a switch from Lana Del Ray and Taylor Swift.

She tries another "Good driving CD" this time, making sure the volume is lower. "White Rabbit" rumbles through the speakers. This song is definitely about drugs, popping pills that make people smaller, or taller, or something.

"Holy crap. I'm gonna get an education."

Finally she settles on one marked Allman Brothers and listens to that. Nothing too excitable there. The opening guitar licks to "Midnight Rider" begin playing, and she turns up the volume and opens the windows, directing the rig from the middle part of Illinois toward Tennessee. With any luck, she'll be in Stone Mountain tonight.

MR. FORSYTHE'S REVISED directions takes her beyond the actual park entrance by about a mile. Curious, she pulls into the trailer park and asks at the office if they have a reservation for her. It's after nine p.m. She really needs to quit driving like it's a job.

"You're Tessa Wiliams?" the woman asks doubtfully.

"Yes."

"Mmmmhmmm," the woman intones. She doesn't wear a name tag. Obviously everyone knows everyone else. She's middle aged, and has frizzy fine fake red hair. Her lip gloss is purple and it's smudged a little.

"And how long you staying?"

"One night, maybe two."

"Mmmmmm-hmmm. Says here, a week." Tessa can hear a loud television behind the thin walls of the office. There's a lot of shooting and sirens on TV.

"A week?"

What the hell could Forsythe be thinking?

"Mmmmmhmmm. Says you want a quiet lot. You gotta dog?" the woman asks suddenly.

"Yes."

The woman crosses Tessa off one lot and puts her way in the back. Instead of five lots around her she'll have one neighbor next to her.

"Yeah, okay. License, license plate number, no dogs off leash. Pick up after them." The woman pushes back from the desk and waits for Tessa to hand print her information.

"Got kids?"

"No." Tessa's head is bent over the paperwork and she glances up to see the woman smirking. "Oh . . . that was a joke?"

The woman shrugs, looking over Tessa's brown, blonde-pink hair.

"Site's paid for a week. If you leave early, let us know."

Tessa sighs and goes to find the lot circled on her handheld map. Guessing from the crude diagram and the fine print she heads straight in and all the way to the back. She veers left and follows this drive a short distance. She can see the bottoms of very large trees here. In the morning she'll look over the site and make sure no dead limbs are about ready to fall on her.

The next morning she's out stretching with Murphy before their run. An older guy wanders over from the camper next door with a cup of coffee in his hand.

"Name's Brett." He holds out his hand. He has no drawl to his voice, like the woman the night before. "In town for long?"

"Not really," Tessa says, retightening a shoe lace.

"Nice dog."

"Thanks."

"I'm here working on a movie set," Brett offers. "Union painter."

"Really? I didn't know they used painters on movie sets."

"Oh yeah. It's a good gig, especially when they wreck one by accident."

"So you just travel all over?"

"Pretty much."

"What's the movie?"

"Well, I'd have to kill ya if I told ya," he jokes.

She laughs.

He leans over and whispers, "'Don't Talk to Strangers.' It's a murder mystery set in Atlanta."

"I thought you were giving me advice." Tessa can tell by Murphy's reaction to her neighbor, he's unconcerned. He wanders to a pile of junk and lifts his leg.

She looks up at the trees. They are fine. She looks over to her left and breathes in a little.

“That’s a cemetery.”

“Yup,” Brett says, wandering over with her.

“Well, why is it so . . . I dunno, trashed?” The stones are every which way, and a blue plastic cup blows over the weedy tan grass. She goes to a stone and wipes the long grass from the face. These are very old graves. 1886.

“I believe it’s a black cemetery.”

Mystified, Tessa turns to him.

“From the slave days.”

“Yeah but these should be cleaned up . . .”

“Did you meet the owners last night?”

“Red hair?”

Brett nods.

“Mmmmhmmm,” he intones.

They both laugh.

“Perhaps this is one of those situations where the folks operated it with care and the kids . . .” He wags his head. “Not so much.”

They regard the stones silently as Tessa removes the blue cup and some other debris.

“Just stay away from that branch of the trailer park over there.” Brett waves his coffee cup, indicating a drive that is across the way. Tessa can see four or five mobile homes. Like permanent renters. “Cops are there every week.”

“Thanks.”

“Don’t mention it. Have a good run. You might just wanna take your truck and run at the park. It’s a lot quieter over there.”

TESSA FOLLOWS BRETT’S advice. She drives in the park, curious about the giant piece of granite that gives the area its name. She reads the information marker. “Second largest piece of exposed granite in the world.”

People are hiking up and down on it.

"Whaddya say, Murphy? Wanna try?"

They follow a younger couple and get started up the slope. According to the info it's eight-hundred-and-fifty feet high. As they climb and course their way around the rock, Tessa is tempted to jog at certain intervals. To her right she notices someone running a little faster—a guy, a few years older than her, running up the mountain with one leg and a crutch. Her jaw drops. He looks back and winks.

She gets to the top and settles on a private rock protrusion and Murphy circles it and lies behind her. Above them she hears a weird sound and looks up.

Flocks of huge birds are circling and calling and wending their way through each other, like threads in the sky.

"Sandhill cranes," the guy with one leg says to her. "They migrate twice a year here."

"That's so awesome."

"Sure, if you wear a hat," he jokes. He's not wearing one either, but he pulls a lime green cycle cap from the back of his shorts. "Have one on me."

"Seriously?" She puts it on.

"Looks good with the pink."

"You're amazing." Tessa looks at his crutch.

"Nah." The guy smiles. "I just don't let anything stop me. Not even my own stupidity. Motorcycle accident. So now I'm healthier than I've ever been. Blessings."

He cranes his neck up to regard the birds.

"Why do they come?" Tessa asks.

"Maybe to watch the Hawks play."

"Hawks?"

"The basketball team."

Tessa feels ridiculous.

"Actually I'm unsure why. Some say there's a magnetic

force in the granite and the birds know where to go from here. They meet up and separate into four different directions, spring and fall. To me, *that's* amazing."

Tessa watches with him.

"Well, I have to get back down," he says after a moment. "Enjoy Atlanta."

Tessa marvels at the way she's meeting so many good people just by putting herself out there, by traveling. By willing to be available to the moment. And the sights she's seeing opens her eyes to the fact that almost wherever she goes, where other people call home, each place seems to have something unique and special. Just like people. Maybe this is why Madeline Sweet is so addicted to adventuring.

Later in the afternoon, Tessa locates the thing called a carillon. A little old lady sits as erect as she can and plays an organ inside a room that is surrounded by glass. Behind her, the music she's playing on the organ breathes through an elaborate series of dampers to produce bell sounds in the tall bronze-looking pipes outside.

Tessa wanders down with Murphy to the walkway. This early on a weekday, very few people are around and she gently and quietly drops some of Aunt Sadie here, with Murphy witnessing. She takes a quick movie so Dan Forsythe can hear the Carillon playing "My Blue Heaven."

CHAPTER 11

TESSA IS MAKING miles for Port St. Lucie, and Mark and Dolly's airpark home. She's anxious, and if she admits it to herself, to be closer to when Dina joins her. *If* Dina joins her. She looks forward to their semiweekly FaceTimes.

She suddenly realizes, this is probably the way Mom feels every Wednesday.

Tessa and Murphy have quickly formed a routine. She tries driving no longer than six hours a day and she tries getting into a campsite no later than four p.m. They always run or walk in the morning. In the evening they investigate where they are staying. She's managed to only have to do laundry three times so far. The first time, thanks to Joe and Marissa.

Mark and Dolly will let her do laundry. Their voices are manic on the phone, each talking over the other, and Tessa is excited to see them too. Mark tells her he's contacted Junior, his son, who's also a pilot. Junior knows the Keys pretty well. Looking at the long drive down to them, Tessa is hopeful Mark or Junior will give her a plane ride, and she can dispose of Aunt Sadie's ashes out to sea.

The airpark is like a golf course. Everyone has a hangar. The lawns are green and wide and open. Little ornamental trees are planted close up to the houses. Tessa sees a silver bullet camping trailer sitting outside their home. It looks brand new.

Mark still has his familiar moustache, but it's gone all white. Dolly seems even shorter than Tessa remembers. She's Sadie size.

"Let's look at you." Mark hugs her and scrubs her hair. "What's this pink and blonde stuff?" He ruffles it.

The head massage feels good. "You can keep doing that."

Dolly turns her and hugs her and then looks her up and down. "Oh good. You don't have any of those piercings. What's that about anyway, the nose things, and the eyebrow things? Wait, open your mouth."

Tessa does.

Dolly dramatically breathes a sigh of relief. "No tongue piecing. Hallelujah!" Her right hand is on her breast and her left hand is up in the air as she talks to the heavens.

Murphy is prancing all around them, his flag-like tail up, waving happily. He noses each of their hands for some attention and then runs, searching the ground.

"Sorry, champ," Mark calls out to him. "If you're looking for a stick, the only trees we have here are the short ones." He suddenly grins. "Loop de loop?"

"Mark!" Dolly slaps him. "Let her settle. My gosh, she just got here. She looks exhausted."

"I drove ten hours." Florida is longer than she thought.

"Oh well, where are my manners?" Mark rolls his eyes. "Maybe a Scotch then? Or a bourbon?"

"Oh for God's sakes, don't mind him. He drives me crazy." Dolly leads them to the house and Mark pairs up with Tessa, walking funny from side to side, making googly eyes, and circling his finger by his temple. He sticks his tongue out sideways, toward Dolly.

"I know what you're doing Mark Tanner, just stop it," Dolly says without turning around.

After dinner the Tanners ply her with all sorts of questions.

"How's Uncle Chuck, the chunk?" Mark asks, lifting his second glass of whiskey to his lips.

Tessa makes a face.

"I figured he'd be a horse's ass."

"Mark!"

"Oh c'mon, Dolly. That guy's been throwing his weight around since the best part of him ran down his father's leg . . ."

"Mark Tanner, behave."

Tessa is laughing at Uncle Marks quips.

"Don't egg him on." Aunt Dolly smiles.

"Your mom holding up okay?" Uncle Mark asks.

Tessa nods.

"She works a lot, doesn't she? I want you to know, if you need anything, anything, you call us."

"Thank you."

She looks out the window. Above all the windows and the doorways are little ledges with Dolly's prized blue plate collections.

The house is immaculate with blues and whites and soft pinks. Lots of windows. Light and airy. And the sound from airplanes occasionally landing and taking off is muffled.

"Eli?"

"He might be out before I get home."

"Seriously?"

"Yeah, the estate lawyer guy hooked Mom up with another lawyer."

"Well, that was all trumped up bullshit egged on by Chuck. Eli no sooner stole your dad's truck as . . ."

Dolly shoots Mark a look of pure whoop ass to shut the hell up.

"I'm just saying, Chuck used his bullshit two-bit county fire chief position to stick it to Eli. Corn pone country bumpkin justice. That's all I'm going to say."

"Well, thank the Christ on that one, Mark Tanner."

Dolly's lips are a thin line as she starts gathering dishes, and Tessa jumps up to help.

"It's okay. I trust you guys. If you want to talk."

"No, honey," Mark says softly as she walks behind him,

he puts his hand on her forearm. "I just want you to know how much you are loved."

Tears spring to Tessa's eyes and she sets the dishes down. She hugs him fiercely from behind. "Thank you."

Tessa stays longer than she intends with Mark and Dolly. Although she's enjoyed meeting new folks, there's nothing like family and home.

She realizes how homesick she is now.

MARK IS OUT at the vomit comet, doing a pre-flight check. His iPod is sitting on the cement and playing old rock and roll.

"Isn't Junior coming today?"

Mark scowls. "Well, he was supposed to."

Tessa watches Mark check the pitot tube in the wing.

She runs her hand softly over the silver foils of the plane. Mark has taken her up every day for nearly a week, showing her the control and speed and acrobatic maneuvering it had. He even let her take the controls in the air.

"I'm flying you to Key West."

Tessa senses something amiss, but she keeps quiet.

"Junior and his clients," Mark hisses.

"Doesn't he fly corporate, or something?"

"Yeah, something," Mark spits out as if he has a bad taste in his mouth.

A tune starts and Uncle Mark shouts, "Bill Haley and the Comets!" He starts boogying toward Tessa and grabs her.

Dolly, who is gardening the flower bed in front of the house, sits back on her heels and claps.

They twist and spin and he leads her impressively. By the time the song is over, they are both winded and laughing. Murphy is prancing all around them, hopping with his two front paws back and forth as if he is dancing too.

"Wow, Uncle Mark, you can rave."

"Ya like that? I used to be quite the ladies' man in my day." He wiggles his thick white eyebrows and twists one corner of his moustache.

"Mark Tanner, you haven't lost a step!" Dolly calls out.

He bows toward her graciously. "Thank you, love."

"Do you think Murphy can go?"

"Why not? We don't have to go so high it will hurt his ears. And I won't do any funny stuff. We'll just fly there, catch a ride. I've got a friend that has a boat."

"Oh, I thought we'd just buzz the water."

"Well, we could, but I might get in trouble." Mark winks. "Besides, it will be nicer from a boat."

Mark didn't even drink the night before the flight. Regulation is twelve hours. He's only been in one accident and he wasn't the pilot. He barely recovered from that one. He told Tessa he even does preflight checks after Junior.

"Just like your rig." Mark nods at her truck and trailer. "You have a check down list, right? I bet you checked it twice every day for a week, didn't you?"

Tessa nods. "Still do."

"Good girl. And if you ever ride with anyone else towing anything, you check it down too. Promise me."

"I promise."

"Well, one last bathroom break, and we're set."

EVERY WATER SPOT is different. As they skim away from the reefs and protected refuge areas, Tessa holds Murphy beside her. The fishing charter guy is drinking beer, but Mark politely refuses. He drinks water. The boat slows and the captain nods to her.

He cuts the engines entirely and they drift lazily in the soft blues and deeper blues.

Tessa unzips the bag. In her mind she's done the ceremony she needs, and she's reticent doing it in front of two older men. So she just softly drops the ashes and watches the heavier ones bubble down below the surface, while the lighter flecks ride on top. She snaps a picture and sends it.

Though the location services are on, Tessa types in, "Key West."

She takes a picture of Murphy. And then one of Uncle Mark and the Cap'n. Uncle Mark is lifting his plastic water bottle and making a goofy face and the captain proudly hoists his Bud Light. She sends this one to her mom.

THE NEXT DAY, Tessa is ready for her westward trip. She has no more excuses to prolong her stay, but it's difficult leaving. She's unsure why.

"Why don't you join me for a week or two?" Tessa looks over at the Airstream.

"Maybe we should try?" Mark nudges Dolly with his hip and elbow.

"Oh, honey." Dolly looks at her, shading her eyes against the sun. "I don't think that's for us. I'm not even sure why we got that."

Mark's face falls, then he turns to Tessa and shrugs with half a smile, as if he doesn't know why either. "We mainly use that for overflow company. And the grandkids enjoy playing house in it . . ."

"Maybe we could fly out and meet you sometime."

"Really? I'd like that a lot."

"I could see us flying out there to meet you more than driving that thing," Dolly admits.

They hug and Tessa is sad to leave. It's nice to have someone see her off and wave goodbye. She doesn't understand why they can't just come along. For some reason she wants the company.

MARK AND DOLLY watch Tessa's rig turn out from the park.

"I swear to god, if anyone hurts that girl, I'll kill them," Mark says.

"I know," Dolly agrees. "I'd want you to."

CHAPTER 12

AS SHE NEARS her first general mail delivery drop, Tessa is excited and nervous. She'd picked out three drops on the pre-trip so her mom would know where to send any snail mail that came for her and maybe, some home treats.

Tessa finds Ottine, Texas by two o'clock and is thrilled to be there before post office closing time. Except, she's circled the two street town twice and can't find the post office.

She sees more cattle thavn people.

She finds one house with a tree growing out of its foundation, and a mailbox.

It looks like a building that is closed up, derelict, and deserted.

Before she can knock on the door an old man that's been watching her parade for the last fifteen minutes says, "Miss Maybelle is gone for the day."

"Is this the post office?"

"Indeed it is, but Miss Maybelle ain't coming back till nine-thirty tomorrow morning. Where'd you come from?"

"Florida."

"Long way for nothing. There's a campground that a way." The man waves in the general direction she first came from.

"Is there anything going on?"

"Well, there's a watermelon seed spitting contest in Luling late June. The Watermelon Thump. Guinness World record is Lee Wheelis. Sixty-eight feet nine-and-one-eighth inch . . . Think you can top that?"

Tessa opens her mouth and shuts it.

"Guess not. Say, you got pink hair?" The man squints.

"Yes, sir."

"I don't think they have a contest for pink hair."

"Probably not." Tessa is desperate to extricate herself but the man with the hunched back and cane saves her the trouble.

"Well, I got things to do." He sets off at a shuffle. "Can't stand around jaw jacking all day."

Thump goes the watermelon.

Once Tessa sets up camp, she is again, the only one in the whole campground. She decides to unhitch the truck and drive down to a sign reading, "Cemetery."

She follows the little paved road till it becomes a dirt road without warning and a short way down, a sign stands next to a pasture gate pointing, "Cemetery." She pulls off the road and pockets her keys. Murphy trails along with her.

On the pasture gate is a sign that reads, "Cemetery open 9 am till 6 pm. Please shut both gates to keep cattle in."

Tessa looks at the two gates and fence rows about three truck lengths apart.

She doesn't see cows and she doesn't see headstones.

Thump.

How can a cemetery be open or closed? Tessa wonders what the fine is for being in the cemetery at six-oh-five p.m. She suddenly gets a fit of the giggles. As disappointed as she is to not have her package today, or having to camp early and stay in Ottine one more day than necessary, this just cracks her up.

"I dunno, Murphy, maybe I'm losing it." She unwinds the wire around the gate, goes through, and carefully winds it back. She repeats the procedure on the next gate.

She is a little skeptical of snakes though and keeps Murphy close to her. They stay on the two track and still Tessa sees nothing but meadow on the left and large swampy trees on the right, the edge of the Palmetto State Park she is camping in.

They walk a couple of football fields and Tessa spies

another cemetery sign pointing to the right. She's unsure why she's drawn to cemeteries. Sometimes she can read history there, and it opens her imagination.

In the meadow is a large ornate, wrought iron enclosed cemetery. The words "Ottine" are etched in the wrought iron in a high arch above its black latched gate.

Tessa suspects there's a lot more people in the Ottine cemetery than out. Three brothers, all died between 1861 and 1865. Maybe the Civil War. Lots of baby deaths in the early 1900s. She strolls for some time among the many old headstones, drinking water and letting her imagination roam. She begins hearing sounds, munching grass, and little huffs and puffs of cattle breaths.

They are grazing just a few yards away, seemingly unaware anyone is in the cemetery until the gate creaks. She whispers to Murphy to keep quiet as they move quickly toward the road. Some of the curious cattle follow. One, much bigger than the rest, has taken a very keen interest and is following faster than Tessa likes, with alert ears forward. She confirms with one look that it's the bull.

She is so focused on getting through the first gate and securing it, she doesn't realize someone is watching her until Murphy barks, his hackles up. She smells the stale old cigar aroma before she sees him.

There, leaning against the side of the Ford Truck, with his arms spread wide on the rails, as if he owns it, is Uncle Chuck.

"Surprise!" he says with artificial glee.

Tessa is holding Murphy back and trying to shush him.

"Well, darlin', the bull or me?"

The bull.

The bull's head is over the first gate, snuffing and snorting. Slowly Tessa walks forward, leashes Murphy at the gate, and then goes through and secures the gate.

"Yeah, you better control that dog. Would hate to euthanize him just because he viciously attacked me." Chuck stands fully and one of his thick hands holds a shotgun. Aunt Sadie's shotgun.

"Think there was only one set of keys?" His eyes narrow in on her. "I found what belongs to me."

He waves her over. He opens up the tailgate and slaps it.

"You and I are gonna have a little talk."

Defiantly Tessa walks to the cab and opens the windows for Murphy. She makes sure he has water, before returning to the rear of the truck. Uncle Chuck's black Chevrolet is parked enough behind that he leans on that hood now. He still holds the shotgun, but it's pointed down now, casually, as if it is a walking stick. His thickness dwarfs it.

"Hop in there. Sit right up there. Old Uncle Chuck wants to hear your side of the story." He's sweating, big beads of sweat mat the sides of his hair down. It's not a good look for him.

She doesn't "hop up there." She leans against the tailgate. It's desolate here. Only the cattle as witnesses. There's nothing else and no one else.

"What story?"

He snorts. "You know what story. Don't play me, *Miss Pink Hair*." He spits. "Bet you're wondering how I knew, eh?" His grinning belies his rage, anger, bitter tone.

Tessa senses his energy like the wind. It's concrete, three dimensional to her. His bluntness and thickness obvious, and his energy tastes like a steely, acidic copper in her mouth.

"I got my ways. Seems more than one person can keep track of you."

"What do you want?" Tessa keeps her voice steady and firm.

She folds her arms over her lower abdomen.

"Go on and sit up there, Missy. Get comfortable. This could take a while."

I doubt it, the way you're sweating.

"I'll start." Uncle Chuck walks over to his passenger side door, opens it, and tosses the shot gun in. He takes a moment to light his half cigar butt, then throws the lighter on the seat. He slams the door shut and returns to her, slapping his hands together.

"Does your momma know about your girlfriend? Your little waitress girlfriend? Yeah. I know about her. And about the lacrosse boy. The garage guy. What? Can't make up your mind? Girl, Boy. Boy girl?"

She stiffens. Before her mom hears it from Uncle Chuck, she'll tell her. He's just trying to bluff her. He's still pacing back and forth in front of his truck, puffing his half phallic stinky cigar.

"There's lots of stuff I know, but what I don't know is . . . what happened to my brother?" he screams in her face.

The cigar is out of his mouth and its heat is very near her cheek.

As shaken as Tessa is, all she can hear is, *"He's afraid."*

Murphy is barking ferociously and pawing desperately to get through the rear slider. He whines and tries to stick his head through the passenger window.

"Shut the hell up you stupid fucking dog!"

He slaps the tailgate next to her.

She doesn't say a word. She closes her eyes and sends her thought to Murphy. *It's okay, Murphy, it will be okay.*

He settles a little, but continues a sporadic, muted whine.

"See I know that Indian, *Josh,* has something to do with it. Benzie County might have shit sheriffs, but I've got contacts all over this country. In the FBI. You ain't got shit. I'm not leaving till I get answers, and there's no one out here, darling, but you and me."

She hates him using the word, darling. She hates it as much as she hates hearing kids her age say "hon" to older people like they were frail or invalid or children.

She annunciates very clearly and very slowly. "I don't remember."

"Yeah." He waves a hand at her. "I'm tired of that story. It might've worked on everybody in the hospital, but it doesn't work with me. You're going to remember, or I'm going to make your brother's life a living hell."

Haven't you already?

"He's the one who took off. Not Eli or Josh."

"Oh. You believe that load of shit, do you? Think Gabe would just leave all of his stuff behind, his girlfriend, his truck, his dog, his wallet? Your brother's in prison doing time for stealing his truck. At least someone else besides me believes that. That's a fact."

"He didn't steal his truck."

"Right. That's why he got caught in it. That's why he got tried as an adult for it."

Tessa clamps her mouth shut. There's a million things she wants to say. It's because of Chuck and his cop cronies in the county and the state that Eli got blamed at all.

Sometimes she wishes she could remember.

His cell phone rings, a tone of Barry White, "Can't get enough of your love, babe."

It's Aunt Deidre. She doesn't need a megaphone, her voice projects. Chuck halfway turns and says, "Yeah. Yeah, babe, I'm here now."

"Did you tell her?"

"I will now. I got it all set up. Yeah. I gotta go."

He turns to her. "Tomorrow you and I are going to a hypnotherapist."

She laughs.

"No. You're going to do this or I'm going to put the

screws to your whole family. This is *my brother* we're talking about. *My* blood. So, if you don't want to put Eli or your mom through more shit and more bankruptcy, you're going to cooperate. Just how selfish are you anyway? It's because of you your mom almost lost her house. That's all your fault. No one else's. Don't think your cobbled-up old Forsythe is going to stop me. I don't give a shit about the inheritance."

He spits. His shirt is soaked. If Chuck does have a heart attack, Tessa is certainly not going to perform mouth to mouth.

The twilight is taking over and the mosquitoes are biting.

"I'm in the campground. We're leaving in the morning. I already got us an appointment in San Antonio." He tosses her something.

It's a patch that reads NAWAC. He stubs his cigar out on the tailgate next to her. "A souvenir of Ottine. Don't go thinking you can sneak out on me like you did Joe. I found you once. I'll find you again. It's just a matter of time. And I'm not giving up. That I swear to you."

He leans over and it's all she can do to not budge from his heaviness. She smells his stench as he whispers in her ear, "Midnight Rider." He slaps the back quarter panel by the tail light and stares one more time through her.

"You don't want those folks having to come find you." He indicates the patch. He gets in his truck, and the springs squeak and the truck tilts to the left. He peels out backward, kicking up dirt and gravel, and roars forward, leaving Tessa and her truck in a choke of dust.

She puts her hand over the white Pegasus unicorn she had drawn on the powder blue part of the truck with paint Brett gave her in Stone Mountain. Below it, on the cream-colored part of the panel with a musical note, is written in brush script, "Midnight Rider" in midnight blue.

Once she gets in her pickup she reads the emblem.

North American Wood Ape Conservancy.

What the hell?

Murphy puts his head in her lap and licks the tears from her chin.

SHE DRIVES FOR hours, hoping to elude any more confrontation with Chuck. She goes to Luling and looks over the fairgrounds where she would not be competing for the Guinness World Record in seed spitting. It starts raining. A torrential rain, the kind of rain that makes rivers out of lines in the gravel in a matter of seconds. Tessa leaps out and shuts the cover over the bed of the truck. She turns home for now, toward the camper.

Uncle Chuck's truck and trailer camp site sits like a big fuck you finger, parked right in the middle, at the first site of the only drive for entrance and exit. The only good thing is he's about ten sites down, not right next to her. Before she enters the camper she makes sure the kayak is dry. She'd stashed it underneath, unsure if she'd try and kayak the San Marcos River by herself.

Once inside, she sages everything: herself, Murphy, every corner of her home, her nest. Chuck had been inside, that's how he got the shotgun. She draws a thunderbird and sticks it up over the interior side of the door. It gives her strength and something positive to focus on. Somehow she falls asleep. Maybe it's the monsoon thundering on the roof, but inside, a cozy and dry place against the harsh pelting rain and winds that occasionally rock the camper. She dreams about worms. Big, puffy, black, Cheetos-like ones and itchy little black fleas. She dreams there's a hundred-and-fifty feral cats in the basement of her camper and everyone is lined up outside her door, willing to help her out and take one home. Somewhere in the middle of the night, in addition to the hard pounding rain, she hears a rumble of a camper pulling right next to her.

Great, it's probably him.

At nine a.m. no one is banging on her door. The rain, if any, has stopped. The wind gusts now and then and kicks droplets out of the trees and onto the roof, sounding staccato beats as if from a prehistoric, giant woodpecker.

Tessa didn't want to worry her mom, but she did call Forsythe when she was at the fairgrounds, before the rain. She only got his voicemail last night. She looks at her phone, no text. No call from him. She finally crawls out of bed. She opens the front door. Stretching, she looks. And looks again. Both ways. Murphy springs out and does his business. Tessa walks all around the camper and cranes to see all the sites she can see.

No black Chevrolet. There is a huge truck and trailer next to her. White, with slide outs. It's opulent and dwarfs her camper by three sizes. Tessa decides, for whatever reason, Chuck is no longer on her. Maybe he got hung up at the Waffle House.

Her package. Suddenly Tessa remembers why she is in Ottine in the first place.

She hears a whirr and in the middle of the road is a familiar scooter. Chris Hooper. He bumps into her tennis shoe with a laugh.

"Well, hi there, young lady. Fancy meeting you here."

"What are you doing in Ottine?"

"Why looking for you of course." Chris grins.

She laughs.

"We have a general delivery."

"So do I."

"Well isn't that something. Have you eaten breakfast yet?"

"No."

"Well, good. C'mon in our rig and we'll get some going."

"This, is you?" she points to the three slide outs.

"You betcha. Wasn't that storm last night something? We pulled into the site with no big trees around it, just like you," he says approvingly.

Cindy sees her through a window, waves, and runs out. They hug immediately, like long lost sisters.

"Isn't this a nice surprise?" Cindy says with a beautiful smile.

"It sure is," Tessa agrees. "Where are you two headed from here?"

"Northern Arkansas. You?"

"New Mexico. Some place called Truth or Consequences."

"Oh, that was named for a TV show."

"Really?" Tessa scrunches her nose. "Why?"

"They wanted a little fame?" Chris shrugs.

She watches as Chris methodically twists from his chair and athletically balances himself against the hand hold by the door so he can manage the steps into the trailer.

"Ladies first!"

"I'll put Murph in my trailer."

"Any friend of yours is a friend of ours."

After breakfast they all pile into the Hooper's crew cab pickup and Tessa directs them to the post office.

"Don't tell anyone, but that post office isn't accessible. Murph and I will wait here." Chris winks from the driver's seat.

The older woman behind the counter looks up with a beaming smile. Most of her white, wispy hair is in a bun and her wire glasses are fastened with a turquoise loop behind her head.

"Miss Maybelle?"

"That I am."

"Package for Tessa Williams?"

"That I have. ID?"

Tessa passes over her driver's license.

"That's you to a Tee." The woman smiles. "A very large man came in here a few days ago and tried to get that package. He related to you?"

"Not by much."

"A most unpleasant fellow. He smelled ripe too. I didn't like him at all."

"Neither do I."

"Well, his name was not on the package and I wasn't about to hand it over. I told him to just fetch you first."

"Thank you."

"Oh, don't thank me, just doing my job."

"Well, I appreciate it."

After Cindy secures their large package, she grins. "I just love getting general delivery. It's like Christmas on the road."

"This is so cool. I can't believe we had the same mail stop."

"What are the chances?" Cindy agrees. "But we do try to hit the smaller out of the way towns. Were you having trouble with someone on the way down? That large fellow Miss Maybelle mentioned?"

"No. No. It's nothing." Tessa stares down at her package.

After the post office, Chris and Cindy offer to help Tessa hook the truck to her camper. Before she backs up the truck, Tessa drags the kayak out from under the camper and stops.

There, inside it, is a brand new leather rifle sheath.

"See a ghost?" Chris jokes, wheeling his chair up to her.

"Whoa!"

She opens it up and pulls out Aunt Sadie's shotgun. There's no note or anything.

"It's not the way I look is it?" Chris is mockingly holding his hands up in the air.

She smiles. "I don't remember placing this here."

"Well, place it somewhere I don't have to see it, willya? Those things give me the heebie jeebies."

She smiles and carefully unlocks her camper, and looks around. Still no sign of Chuck.

She returns and places the kayak in the bed of the truck. She shuts the tailgate, but leaves the cover open so she can see the mark Paul had installed on the inside of the tailgate. It lines up the hitch and the ball. Tessa can't quite get the distance between the two matched. Sometimes it takes her three or four times of leaving the driver seat and checking just how close she is to have the ball directly under the tongue of the trailer where it needs to be.

Chris, his wheelchair spotted to the driver's side so Tessa can see him in the mirror, holds his fist up. "There it is! You're dead on line." He then removes a tape measure and instructs her to place the dumb side at the rear of the tire. "Now pull it back till you're in line with where your ball needs to be for the hitch. Got it?"

She nods.

He throws her a two by four from his wheelchair's front basket. "Now, when you're by yourself, measure that same distance, eyeball where your rear tire is going to back up, and place that two by four where it needs to be to stop the truck.

"He's handy that way." Cindy beams, hugging him.

"Got a tape measure?"

Tessa shakes her head.

"Take that one, I've got two more."

"I can buy one."

"Don't be silly. To tell the truth, he has four of them," Cindy says.

"A little souvenir to remember us by."

Just as Tessa shuts the cover over the truck bed, they all hear a rumble.

"Uh-oh," Chris says. "If that storm coming in has wind anything like last night, Cindy and I better get the awning down and this chair inside. If I were you, I'd wait out the big part of the storm. Take off when it dissipates. Don't leave without saying goodbye. If you're here tonight, we'll have dinner." He grins.

THE RAIN POUNDS on. Cindy is right: receiving the package is like Christmas. Letters and cards from Billy, Dina, and Paul are on top. Eli wrote too. Her mom's envelope is really thick, it must be a really long letter; she puts all those aside because she smells her mom's homemade chocolate chip cookies. Two zip lock bags full. "Put in freezer" note says. There's a long official-looking letter from Mr. Forsythe. In little old man chicken scratch scrawl on the front is written "no rush." She sets it on top of the other letters. These she can open at her leisure since the hard rain is still not letting up.

Her mom included some tea, some books, chocolate, nuts, and real black licorice from England. She even packed a gift bag for Murphy with his name on it and a big bow. Murphy immediately takes notice of this and smells it. Her mom has splurged. The books though, Mom must not have remembered all the stuff under the cushions that Tessa has yet to look at.

Tessa gleefully opens the chocolate chip cookies and throws Murphy a homemade doggie cookie from his treat bag.

She starts sifting through her letters. Dina's first. She had written a long letter with a little poem attached, "Tessa's Motorhome Cantata." Dina's graceful, cursive handwriting, an art form lost among their peers, flows over special woven, beige paper. Expensive. Dina had taken her time, instilling thought into everything about this letter, right down to a soft, aromatic scent. Tessa can almost hear Dina's lyrical voice singing or chanting the verses she'd dovetailed with Tessa's current journey and their relationship.

Dina is highly intelligent and clever that way. She's a scientist and a psychology major, but neither of those had stopped her from entering the same art contest as Tessa.

Tessa's wood cut print showed her mother sitting, her hair then in a long braid, arms casually over her knees as she watched two children playing in a schoolyard. She'd taken a black-and-white photograph of her mom, using an old-fashioned film camera. Tessa had been about twelve and her mom agreed to pose for her. The wood cut print received honorable mention, not bad for a freshman.

Dina's charcoal drawing of a nude man frontal reaching for a nude woman, her back to the artist, received first place. Dina just had a natural knack for things like that.

One time they both entered a poetry slam.

As difficult as it was for Tessa to write a poem about losing her twin for an unknown amount of time, it was even more difficult to speak it. People politely clapped.

When Dina got up, she rocked the house.

She pulled her long blond hair up into a twist and she rocked back and forth from one leg to another with her voice loud and insisting they listen and when she ended with, "Yer balls of blood . . ." the room was standing and whistling and she won the slam, hands down.

Afterward, as they shared a beer outside at one of the quiet tables, Tessa said, "I don't know how you do it. You can do anything."

Dina laughed." I just give them what they want. It's a no brainer."

"So, you don't live this stuff?"

Dina shrugged. "A little. No. Not that much really. People are predictable. The slam is run by guys who want to think women want to suck them off so a poem like that rocks their world. It's stupid really. Let's get outta here before one of them makes a pass at us, okay?"

"But like the Art Contest . . ." Tessa asked as they walked.

Dina waved her hand. "It's a game. I go online, see who the judges are, their likes and dislikes and fill the void. If it's poetry I write like them. If it's art, I draw like them. I like to see if they'll take the bait. And so far they do, every time. Poetry, if it gives the guys a hard on, you've won."

Tessa never had a man's cock in her mouth and she isn't so sure she ever wants that. The very idea . . . but, according to Dina, that's all men want and they will follow you anywhere.

Tessa just wants Dina following her everywhere, and so far, that hasn't been a problem.

The poem is lengthy and whimsical; Dina has married their actual lives together with a mystical one and it ends with them someday living together. Tessa falls back on the bed with the letter on her chest, in bliss. She is sure she will treasure this one letter alone for the rest of her life.

Next she opens Eli's letter. He's in great spirits. The new lawyer went to court after hiring a highly respected private investigator, a former state police detective the judge knows, and the judge has agreed to review the private investigator's findings. Huge news. Tessa is elated.

She opens Paul's letter next. It's written on garage notepad paper. Paul's Automotive. Wow. She didn't know he owned the garage, she thought he just worked at it.

> I take very seriously all you've chosen to share with me. I know I reacted poorly at first. I apologize. I asked you to be honest and you were. You're the type to wear your heart on your sleeve and I do care about you a lot. I can't pin it on any one

> thing. You just mean a lot to me. Maybe we're not meant for each other, but I'd like it if you would still consider me a friend.

Wow. She thought she'd never hear from him again after she told him everything. She had to be honest with him. As cute as he was, she couldn't sleep with him.

Billy's letter. She dreaded this one. But better to rip the band-aid off now. She isn't very careful opening this envelope. As suspected, he blames everything on Dina and writes he has been played. He admits visiting her mom! Oh, for fucks sake. Really? Her mom never mentioned that. Wait till the next Mommy Call. He ends the letter with, once Dina doesn't need Tessa, he may or may not be around. As if.

Her mom's letter fills her in on all the neighborhood news, which they've already shared on the iPad in the once a week sessions. The best newest news is Holly called, asking about her and will be home for a visit in the fall, so they can catch up then.

Mr. Forsythe's letter packet is full. It has some extra gas cards, written info on official contacts along the way, should any more trouble arise, some interesting facts about the places she is going next and the procedure for a smooth customs crossing at the border.

There. All her box is done, except for the gift.

The small box is heavy for its size and ornate, a grey box with darker designer grey lines in overlay, tied with a gold bow.

Tessa carefully unties the bow.

Inside, wrapped in heavy paper and cotton swathing is a smaller box. Inside that box, a gold ring with a small, secondary crescent band arching upward on a slight angle, encircling a beautiful, small diamond.

The inscription reads, “With love, Dina.”

Tessa realizes she isn’t breathing. Her heart burns and happy tears fill her eyes.

She’s bursting to share this enormous news with someone. Unable to tell her mom, who doesn’t approve; she certainly can’t run next door and show the neighbors. Eli would understand. She sighs and holds the moment to herself.

Their tummies full, Tessa’s heart glowing, the incessant rain lulls her to sleep.

TESSA STORES HER letters under the sofa seat with the travel books and DVDs and old photo albums. She thumbs through the old albums, trying to take her mind off the fact she would like to run next door and show off her ring, but then she’d have to explain everything. She can’t call Dina, because she won’t be out of work till midnight. Additionally, part of her is nervous that Uncle Chuck is lurking somewhere nearby, ready to pounce again. Perusing the photo albums settles her jumbling, tumbling mind.

Murphy lies patiently at her feet, his dry warmth snuggled against her, during the second monsoon. She chooses the photo album filled with black-and-white pictures, figuring they are the earliest. Aunt Sadie and Uncle Percy on their wedding day, best man and maid of honor beside each of them. The maid of honor is as tall as Percy.

Relatives and little kids she doesn’t know.

Then there are old pictures of The Grand Canyon. Tessa recognizes the fabled dimpled series of mountains. She’s always wanted to try painting an image of these same mountains with purple hues of watercolor. Mule deer. Much smaller than Northern Michigan ones.

She pages through and realizes some of these pictures are the route she is covering. Every now and then different couples join them, as if they'd just met up at a campground, or on the road.

Sadie and Percy were sure hearty travelers. First in a wood-paneled station wagon. Sadie smiling, with the rear tailgate door open, on her tummy, face in her hands, a nice fit for her, but what about Percy? The back didn't look long enough for him. Maybe they put a board out for him.

Oh, there's the barn on North Manitou. Wow, there were more buildings, and roads, and houses. An old shipwreck still visible.

Traverse City had just a paved two-lane along the water, and motels. Everything seems familiar but looks different.

She finds a color album starting in the sixties. The tall lady and shorter man couple. He has glasses. Tessa opens up the black-and-white album. The tall lady with a different man. No. It's the same man. He has no glasses and a lot more hair. The young twenty-something version.

Percy with dark hair in the black and white and this fellow. Washboard tummies, just like Cousin Joe. All men must have them, Tessa sighs.

Tessa looks from the color photo to the black and white. Then she pages back to the wedding photo. It's the same couple, just not married yet.

Tessa has breezed through another set of wedding pictures because it isn't anyone she knows, except Sadie and Percy. Then she sees Sadie and Percy are at their wedding, their best friends.

Wow, they sure hung with that couple a lot. Those people even came out to visit them, in some desert place. A motel with a couch outside in front of it. Deserty-looking mountains behind. The motel looks flat and new and kind of kitschy her mom would say. Men with cowboy hats and boots, one foot up on a half barrel, another foot up on a water trough.

Tessa returns to the color album. There's a loud knocking at her door.

She hasn't noticed but the rain has let up and now she's suddenly frightened.

Uncle Chuck? The pounding continues.

"Tessa! It's Cindy." Tessa opens the door. "Want some dinner?"

"Is it that late?" Tessa realizes it's getting dark. "I guess I got lost in the photo albums."

"Is that what your box held?"

"No." Tessa smiles. "Letters, but I burned through all them and then I received these." She holds up one of the bags of chocolate chip cookies.

"Dessert!" Cindy squeals and her eyebrows pop up over the rim of her glasses. "It's finally quit raining, for a moment there, we thought we might all have to move to higher ground. Flooding."

"Wow, the high water being an issue never even occurred to me."

"In the National Parks they try to keep an eye out for folks, but in some of these smaller places, you're left on your own. The San Marcos is behaving for us."

"Have you ever heard of this?" Tessa shows Cindy the NAWAC patch. Cindy doesn't notice the new ring on her finger, and that's okay.

"I can't say that I have, but bring it over, Chris will be interested in seeing it."

CHAPTER 13

DINA FACETIMES HER while she's on the road.

"I can't FaceTime, I'm driving."

"God, you're beautiful, the way the sunlight is hitting you as you drive. Can't you just prop it up somewhere?"

Murphy is sitting in the passenger seat and looks at her with an "I ain't budging" look.

"Mmm, lemme try this." She pops Dina into the old-fashioned ashtray. "If I hit a bump, this isn't real stable, just call back."

"I've got news for you and I wanted to see your face when I told you."

"K, hit me!"

"I dropped Xander."

Tessa is speechless.

Dina claps her hands and laughs. "You should so see your face. Baby. You can pick up your lower jaw, don't let it hit the steering wheel."

"I just can't believe you're not sleeping with him anymore."

"You're way more loyal than he's ever going to be. Besides. You're a hard worker."

"That's why you're dating me? Because I'm a hard worker?"

"No. I'm dating you because you're so damn fine in bed."

"Dina!"

"I'm dropping Xander and focusing on you because you're a hard worker."

Tessa smiles.

"Besides, who else would take a crazy ass trip by

themselves across the country? You've got guts. I love that about you."

"Thanks, it's fun really, except for Chicken-butt Chuck. Dina, all the people on the road are really cool. Who knew? It's way easier than I thought. The only bad thing is I'd like to be sharing all these sights with you."

"Well, we're just going to have to take our own camping trip next year."

"Really? You promise? What about school?"

"By then I'll know if I'm accepted here for my Masters, then I have a little time."

"Awesome. Baby? I really have to concentrate on traffic, I'm driving around San Antonio, but can we talk tonight?"

"Count on it. I love you, Tessa Marie!"

"I love you, Dina Kay!"

"Bye . . . Kisses!"

Tessa makes a kissy face at the phone before it goes dark.

And sighs a deep happy sigh.

"How 'bout that Murph? I got a sweet, sexy woman!"

Murphy yawns and looks out the window.

WHEN TESSA FOLLOWS the GPS directions of her next ash drop, she rechecks her co-ordinates and itinerary. The hot tub spa place in Truth or Consequences looks like a decrepit old motel. There's some driftwood out front of a dirt circular drive and a couch, dragged from somewhere. It looks vaguely familiar, but not.

The building has seen better days. The peeling turquoise-and-pink paint, and cigarette butts around the edges of the site.

She walks into the small office and a girl with purple streaks in her blonde hair and double rings in her nose looks up. She's been toying with her hair, she doesn't stop as she asks, "Hot Springs? Half hour or an hour?"

Tessa must look lost so the girl points to a chalkboard over her head.

"Welcome to T or C hot springs. Soothing natural hot springs. ½ hour private room soak $4, 1 hr. /$8." All the letters are in different chalk colors and the one slash two in half hour are blue, orange, and red.

"Uhm, half."

"Four dollars. Gotta towel? Cause that's more."

"I have a towel."

The girl looks out and see's Tessa's rig. Murphy is poking his head out the window.

"No dogs, k? There's shade out back, I think you can park your whole thing there. Make sure he has water, k? I don't like folks who abuse animals."

Tessa nods.

The girl gives her an old-fashioned motel key, reading, "Coynes Resort" on a leather tag, with a ring hole for the key, Room 4.

"It's down and to the left." The girl points to her right.

Tessa is a little creeped out but she does find a shady spot for the rig and Murphy. She leaves the windows open and a nice breeze blowing through.

Murphy doesn't whine and it's only going to be a half hour.

She opens the door to the room and it's surprisingly clean and efficient with a newer wicker chair, a shower, and new bamboo mats with Asian accents. Drinking water with ice just placed there and a lemon slice floating on top. She brought her bathing suit, but once she opens the door to the hot springs she realizes it's unneeded. A huge rope with a knot hangs from the ceiling to an easy reach just above the water. She walks down the two large cement steps into the pool and hangs onto the rope. It's deep enough to submerge her whole body, but if she gets too hot she can pull herself up by the thick rope and sit on one of the cement steps. The rope reminds her of something off a pirate's ship.

The thermal bath is nothing short of delicious. Whatever natural minerals are in the water soothe every road weary ache in her body. Who knew this was waiting behind the façade outside?

Tessa is jolted from her total relaxation by a knock on the door.

"Five minutes, k?" the girl says.

Tessa hasn't done the ashes. She reaches up to the top step and brings them down. She's gotten lost in the thermals, even the traffic outside on the front road, and children playing far off somewhere, the in and out of the hot springs mesmerizes her and she gently releases the ashes to the out portal and watches them drift into the sunlight outside.

Sighing, grateful for the relaxing waters, she climbs out and wraps the towel around her.

This is getting a five star in her memory book.

SHE LETS MURPHY out to run around and sees she has a call from Forsythe.

"Chuck reappear?" he says without a hello.

"No."

"Good. I think he's a man of reason."

Tessa is doubtful. "He kind of threatened my whole family and Murphy."

"I believe his . . . excitement . . . is toned down."

"I don't know how you do it, Mr. Forsythe, from Michigan. I do appreciate everything. Thank you."

"You're more than welcome, Tessa. From here on out I really believe you should have no more trouble, but if you do, do not hesitate to call. Even though it might seem like I'm not responding, rest assured I am. You are performing a vital service. Never doubt that. Did you read any of the additional info on the trailer under the cargo seat?"

Tessa's heart races as she instantly remembers Great Aunt Sadie's journal entry. "Yes."

"Good. You received all the information you need for your Canadian crossing?"

"Yes, everything. All of Murphy's vaccines. And I have a copy of everything, like my passport."

"Excellent. Will anyone be joining you?"

"Maybe. I thought my college friend, Dina. Just for a little while."

"I understand the Canadian Rockies are visually stunning. It will be nice to share those with someone."

Tessa smiles. "Thanks, Mr. Forsythe. Thanks for not being angry about that."

"Angry? This is a long trip. You should have someone join you. Take care, Tessa. Let me know if you need anything."

"I will."

"Just one more thing. Does anyone else, besides your mother, know your travel plans?"

Dina.

"Not really, Mr. Forsythe, I just keep 'em guessing."

"Excellent. Keep up the good work."

Wow. He was surprising her more and more each time she spoke with him.

AFTER THE HOT springs, Tessa really just wants to relax. The girl with the purple hair tells her about Elephant Butte. Although the water in the reservoir is way down because of the drought, kayaking with Murphy is wonderful and easy.

It's Mommy Call night.

Her mom doesn't answer. Not even on the second and third try. That's unusual.

Tessa's reservoir kayaking ran a little late, but her mom usually stays awake till eleven Michigan time.

Tessa frowns. She messages, *Are you at the movies tonight?*

Nothing.

Tessa begins dinner and checks the phone every so often.

Tonight she's grilling veggies and a small piece of pork loin she's marinated.

"Smells good," a woman calls out from the fifth wheel a few sites over.

Her fifth wheel is even bigger than Chris and Cindy's. And she must have a washing machine because her clothes are hanging on a self-made clothesline. All the clothes look theatrical. No truck is on site, just the fifth wheel. The woman strolls over.

She has on cut-off shorts, beautiful sandals, a light sweatshirt that's been strategically ripped at the arms and neck and hanging loosely on her. She has pretty blonde hair and beautiful brown eyes.

She sticks her hand out. "Cheryl."

Murphy comes right up to her, wagging his tail.

"Tessa and Murphy."

"What a beautiful name, Tessa." Cheryl smiles up at her. She bends down and pets Murphy. "And what a cutie patootie you are, you handsome boy."

Murphy runs and finds his cloth rabbit. He flips it up in the air and catches it and looks expectantly at her.

She laughs and claps. "Show off."

Murphy wags his tail.

She turns to Tessa. "Wanna come over later for a campfire? My boyfriend should be back in an hour or so."

"Sure." Tessa notices Cheryl has a tongue ring. Dolly would be having a fit. Cheryl also wears a gold ring on her thumb and a gold bracelet. She has a beautiful diamond on an ankle bracelet. It twinkles colors in the sun.

"You must have a washer in your rig?"

"A washer and a dryer. I'm a featured performer on tour so it's imperative my stuff is cleaned every night."

"Wow. Is that a good living?"

"Oh, yeah, pay cash for everything and I plan to retire by the time I'm forty." She leans over and whispers, "Which is in five years, but don't tell anyone."

Tessa grins.

"Is it just you and your dog?"

"Yes, but I have a friend joining me in a couple of weeks."

"It must get lonely."

"Not too much." Tessa thinks of Mark and Dolly and wonders if Mark will fly out to see her. He said he might.

"Well, I admire you. Good for you. See you in about an hour. When the red truck pulls in, give us a few minutes to get the campfire going."

BEFORE GOING OVER to Cheryl's, Tessa tries her mom one more time, even though it's after midnight, Michigan time. Tessa begins wondering who she can call to check on her mom.

She realizes she's feeling concern and protective, all the things she huffs and becomes impatient with when her mom expresses those same things for her or Eli. These sensations don't sit very well, and she begins to understand some of her mom's reactions. Reluctantly, she pockets the phone and heads over to the little fire she sees between the rig and the big red four-door Ford.

Dean, the boyfriend, is about twenty-five years old. He has that puppy energy that all young guys have when they're in love. He waits on both of them, refusing to let either of them get out of their chairs for a drink or a snack. He hangs on every word Cheryl says, and has a difficult time looking anywhere but in her direction.

When he fetches more wood and is out of hearing distance, Cheryl sighs. "He's a sweet boy and all, but it's not long term. He's already proposed three times. I'm not the marrying kind. At least not yet and not with him. Although he's fun. And obedient. Love that. Have him trained right out of the gate."

"I think he adores you."

"Mmm and I think he's precious."

Dean reappears only to hear that last part and his grin widens. He sits at Cheryl's feet and she rubs his head affectionately.

"I'm your number one man," he murmurs, his eyes closed, as she massages his head.

"So tell us about Tessa." Cheryl looks at her.

"Oh, there's not much to tell, just a girl and her dog traveling around the US and Canada, spreading Great Aunt Sadie's ashes."

"No shit?"

"No shit. Nobody else in the family wanted to do it, and the inheritance doesn't get divided until all the appointed stops are accomplished."

"Holy crap. How long is that going to take?"

"Actually I'm two thirds of the way through, this part. I still have to go east when I return to Michigan." *Thanks a lot, Uncle Chuck.*

"Where do you go from here?"

"Some place called Gila Cliff Dwellings, the Gila river."

"Oh yes. That's by Silver City."

"She knows her geology," Dean says, his eyes still closed. Cheryl smiles.

"Geography."

"Yeah, that."

"See what I mean?" Cheryl mouths as Dean's head rolls all around under her expert massaging hands. *Wanna swap?"* She nods over at Murphy.

Tessa looks down, trying hard not to laugh, shaking her head no.

"Ask her what she does," Dean says to Tessa. Suddenly he's awake and his eyes are open and he's very animated.

"Dean. We're not supposed to mention that."

Dean leaps up and hands Tessa a lighter. "Go ahead. Read it."

The lighter has a photo of a much more made up version of Cheryl on it, thick black eyelashes, model's make up and poofy hair, and a huge bust.

"Voluptuous Vanna eighty-eight inches of Double D's!"

Cheryl shakes her head.

"He's so not supposed to do that."

"Wow. So they pay you to . . ."

"Dance. I charge them airplane flights and drive. Make bank. Tell you I'm socking it away."

"She's my sugar mama," Dean says proudly.

"Yes, well, Sugar Mama doesn't like it when you do that."

Dean frowns. "I'm just proud of you."

"Ya wanna see 'em?" Cheryl asks, and before Tessa can release a sound, Cheryl lifts up her loose-fitting sweatshirt, and there in God's glory are eighty-eight inches of Double D's staring at her.

Tessa automatically closes her eyes.

Dean is laughing so hard he's rolling on his side.

"Uhm, not that they're not great. They're . . ."

"Huge!" Dean laughs.

"Did you smoke some pot when you got the wood?" Cheryl asks him.

"Maybe a little."

"Goof. They are huge. And as soon as I'm done with this kind of thing, they're getting downsized big time."

"That's gotta hurt your back."

"It does and I'm tired of not being able to sleep on my stomach. It's the little things you miss the most. Yours are perfect, by the way." Cheryl smiles.

"I couldn't do what you do."

"I saw you painting at your camp site. Now that's something I'd love to be able to do. Would you show me some of your work tomorrow? We have to shove off for Texas, but we're not leaving till noon."

Dean has fallen asleep on top of Cheryl's feet. Murphy rests against Tessa's leg; the picture is not lost on either of them.

"Sure," Tessa agrees, sharing a smile with Cheryl.

THE NEXT MORNING, she receives a text from her mom.

Sorry about last night. We will try for tonight.

The tone of the whole message is off. The wording is unlike her mother and Tessa begins worrying that Uncle Chuck might be switching gears. Since Forsythe somehow got him to back off, maybe Uncle Chuck is harassing her mother. He might even go after Dina. Josh, she is sure, can pretty much kick Uncle Chuck's butt.

She's debating whether to call Dina, or maybe even Paul, when Cheryl walks over.

"Hey, kiddo, we're just about ready to blow this pop stand. I've got Dean ironing my clothes and hanging them up."

"I dunno, Cheryl. Seems like you have the whole package with Dean. Be hard to give that up."

"Yes, the houseboy aspect is sort of appealing, but it's difficult maintaining a stimulating conversation. The only thing geology and geography have in common are the G and the Y, throw a U in there and you've got My Guy."

"There's the whole geo thing."

They smile.

"Let's see your art."

Tessa's not as timid to show her paintings as she is to share details about herself. Somehow Cheryl sees Tessa through the pictures.

"Oh, wow. This one of the guy and his plane just jumps out. His eyes and smile really pop. You captured his soul."

"That's my Uncle Mark."

"Has he seen this yet?"

"No. I took a picture of him and then painted this in Texas."

"It's beautiful. Did you do the horse on the side of your truck also?"

Tessa nods.

"You have talent, sweetie. The big rig guys would pay you good money to paint emblems and decals on their trucks. You could do motorcycle tanks. The sides of airplanes. Would you . . . would you take a picture of me?"

Cheryl looks at her so intently, Tessa agrees.

They set up in an empty campsite, Cheryl sitting on top of a picnic table with Elephant Butte behind her. Tessa carefully focuses on what Cheryl wants most: Her eyes.

They exchange numbers and just like that, Tessa has made another road friend.

CHAPTER 14

TESSA MAKES CAMP at City of Rocks State Park, following Cheryl's advice. It's about seventy miles to the south of the Cliff Dwellings so Tessa plans on making a day of heading up the twisty road to Gila. Cheryl also warned her dogs aren't allowed, so Tessa grabs the service pack. It would be a long, hot day for Murphy to stay at camp.

The City of Rocks campsites are primitive, but beautiful.

The day before, when she had pulled in, she drove the entire circle, trying to find a flat site on the west side, so she could watch the sunset. No one was around, or so it seemed. She found one north of the windmill used to supply energy to the well providing fresh water for campers.

Just as she levels the trailer, she hears voices and laughter above her.

A few heads stick up, and some kids her age wave.

"Don't use the trash bin," they call out as they laugh and take off.

She's forgotten about it till this morning.

There, in the bottom of the garbage bin, is a paper plate with the remains of about twenty self-rolled, cigarette butts.

She removes the paper plate. She sticks her garbage bag in and takes the plate back to her campsite.

She unrolls the golden tobacco and sniffs it. Bits of pot are mixed in. Dina would love this. She smiles and cleans the tobacco. She sifts the pot out of the twenty or so butts and comes up with enough for one nicely rolled joint. She doesn't smoke, but she saves it for her meeting with Dina in California, before they are even close to crossing the US-Canadian border.

On the top of the rocks she leaves a big thank you note and a sketch of the sunset the night before.

THE DRIVE TO the Gila Cliff dwellings goes up and up and up through mountain pines and a long adventurous road. The truck seems to love being free of the camper and roars up the road like an un-tethered horse.

Murphy's pack actually has a dual purpose: it carries their water and his treats. Tessa has her own pack for extra water and food. She leashes Murphy in the shade as she begins exploring the caves. They've developed a ritual on their hikes and he seems to know the difference between a run and an exploring adventure. Where there's a chance of crowds, they stay close. If it's just a few people, Tessa leashes him in a shady spot and is not gone for very long or very far.

She leaves him with water and enters the area to the Gila Cliffs dwellings.

Once she is above and can see through the arch openings, she looks out over the vista and sees Murphy lying down and gazing up at her. She waves and he wags his tail. The huge dome arches are magnificent, and the series of kivas connected by walkways thrill her.

She walks up some wooden steps and places her hand on a large smooth boulder and stops. The energy of generations of people putting their hands on this same boulder and moving on into the kiva jumps up through her palm and into her arm and shoulder. She looks down her arm and is instantly connected to the people who lived here a very long time ago and mysteriously vanished after taking the time to build these cathedral-like dwellings.

"It's a long way to go for water," says an older woman behind her. She's stocky and strongly built, her dark hair just beginning to grey, and her dark eyes smile. She indicates the river far below.

"I'm sorry. I didn't mean to hold up the line."

A slimmer woman behind the stocky woman smiles and waves good-naturedly. "No worries. Enjoy the moment. I will."

The woman with the intense blue eyes and slightly auburn hair is aware of Tessa's hand on that rock. They're both wearing "Life is good" T-shirts, only the older woman's T sleeves are cut off, so it's more like a tank. Her arms look strong, like they are used to physical labor.

"Awesome boulder, eh?" She pats it with affection.

"Are you from Michigan?"

"Yes I am. How could you tell?"

"The eh?"

The woman chuckles. "You too?"

Tessa nods.

"That your dog out there?"

"Yes."

"Handsome and well behaved. Wish we could have brought ours, but sometimes the parks are funny that way."

"Yes, he's a big help to me."

Tessa climbs inside the kiva to make room for the women.

The older woman closes her eyes and replicates Tessa's posture with the rock. "Imagine all the generations who have ever touched this rock both present and beyond. I've waited far too long to feel this again."

The older woman opens her eyes and breathes a deep sigh, making room for the younger woman behind her. The woman with the auburn hair takes her time as Tessa and the older woman climb around and investigate further into the caves.

"We just came from the Chiricahua Mountains. Before that, Sedona, Grand Canyon, and Zion."

"I'm supposed to go to the Grand Canyon and Zion."

"Supposed to?"

"I'm spreading ashes," Tessa whispers.

She's unsure why she trusts this woman, but she does. It's obvious the two women are a couple, because when the other woman joins them, she grabs her hand and kisses her.

"This is just the way you described it. Awesome."

The dark woman breaks into a wide smile in response.

"I'm Alex and this is Ruth," the older woman says.

"Tessa . . . and Murphy."

"Nice to meet you. Which direction did you arrive from?"

"South. I'm camping at City of Rocks."

"Just where we are headed. I was there long ago. Is it still primitive? No electricity?"

"Just water."

"Is it over run with folks?"

"No, surprisingly not."

"Maybe we'll see you later."

"That would be great."

AT THE GILA River, just after she's snapped a picture of the ashes for Dan Forsythe, Tessa stumbles over a pinyon pine cone. She picks it up and peruses its shape. The seeds inside. The heft of it.

She smiles and puts the pine cone in her pack. And then looks around again.

This is the picture. This is the place in the journal, Tessa is sure of it. A forked pinyon pine, looking exactly like the one in the picture. The flat rock just to the right of it. This is where Percy and Sadie made love, under a pine tree, along this river. Anyone could have stumbled upon them. The park literature clearly states the Gila Cliff dwellings became a national monument in 1907. Sadie and Percy arrived in 1954.

"Wow. You two are much more daring than I'd ever be."

She smells her hands with the scent of the pine cone still on them. Murphy laps from the river, waiting for her. Tessa crouches, and he comes over to her.

"If there really is no such thing as time, maybe Aunt Sadie and Uncle Percy are here. Maybe the Pueblans are still here. Whaddya think, Murphy?"

Tessa refuses to refer to the inhabitants of this region by the Spanish name the park uses, Mogollan. The Pueblans were here before any Spanish Governor arrived.

Murphy wags his long black, flag-like tail, grinning.

"Yeah. I know. I can't quite wrap my head around the whole quantum physics thing either. If our lives are just little worm lines in a bigger reality that we can't see, then everybody is supposed to be existing at once."

Tessa closes her eyes. Everything seems still. For the briefest moment she sees Aunt Sadie and Uncle Percy in their young bodies, full of love and sweetness.

She sighs deeply.

Her phone rings and it's her Mom FaceTiming her.

Even though her mom's eyes are dark, she is grinning from ear to ear.

"Tessa! Fantastic news. Eli is going to be home by the time you return. Mr. Forsythe's friend successfully argued for early release. I'm sorry I wasn't available, but I went to the hearings and I didn't want to call before I knew for sure."

"I'm just relieved everything is okay. Uncle Chuck is being okay?"

"Oh, he's not happy at all, but Mr. Forsythe has something over on him, that's for sure."

"Mom, you won't believe this."

Tessa flips the optics on the phone.

"Aunt Sadie and Uncle Percy were at this exact same spot. I have an old black-and-white photo of them here."

She spares her mom the other details.

"Isn't that awesome?"

"I'm so proud of you, darling. Are you sure you're safe?"

"It's been so cool meeting new people. Everyone has been really kind. I think I've made some new friends."

"That's beautiful, darling." Her mom yawns. "I'm sorry, it's been a complicated and chaotic couple of days, but I promise to speak with you again soon, okay, sweetie?"

"You bet, Mom. I love you."

"Love you. Love you, Murphy."

Murphy, sitting right next to Tessa, wags his tail. Tessa takes his paw and waves bye to her mom.

She drives into the City of Rocks campground and sees Ruth and Alex strolling hand in hand. A black dog with white on his chest and a funny shade of a smile on his face is walking next to them. They wave to her, and she stops.

"Hungry?" Alex asks.

"Famished."

"Judging from the color of your truck, I believe we camped two sites south of you. How 'bout coming over in a half hour? We'll catch the sunset together."

"Thanks. What can I bring?"

"Do you have any fruit?"

"Yes."

"Awesome, it's a date."

Before walking to dinner, Tessa pulls out the journal with the pinyon pine in the background. She hadn't seen the edge of the water, but there it is. Her aunt had written:

> *Some years the Gila will dry up completely, like when the German Prisoners of War tried to escape in 1944. Their plan was perfect. They even had made and tested a collapsible kayak right under their*

captor's noses, but the Gila River in Arizona, when they arrived, was just a dried up rut that year. They were all eventually caught.

This year the river is resounding and beautiful as Percy and I nap.

Tessa's imprint of the picture in her mind's eye had been spot on, save for the river. If she hadn't stumbled on the pine cone she never would have known. She never would have looked back and seen that specific sight. For a moment, she's slipped into Sadie's heart and soul as easily as slipping someone else's shirt over her head and fitting it against the skin of her body.

Does she dare hope this is the kind of love she shares with Dina? Do they?

CHAPTER 15

TESSA JUMPS UP to expressway 40 to 64 toward the Grand Canyon. Although Alex and Ruth had strongly recommended going to Moab and the Canyonlands and Arches National Parks, the closer she gets to San Francisco, the closer she is to Dina's arrival. Her plans are to stay the course for her ash drops at the Grand Canyon and Zion.

The Grand Canyon is much more than photographs can express, but then photographs cannot translate the air, or the depth. Tessa wonders, if all these professional photographers and artists have failed in capturing the Canyon's essence, how can she even hope to try?

Still, she waits for the dinner hour, when most trails become less hectic.

She hikes to a lookout south of the fabled dimpled pyramids, a sight that can even be seen from space. A corridor of symmetrically eroded rock monuments marching like sentinels from the southwest to northeast.

She quickly sketches in the rough shapes and adds the foreground of the protruding rock edifice on her side of the canyon with the canopy of the tree draping over her.

She has never attempted 3D. Using this sketch as a blueprint, she can try different mediums. On the Internet, she's seen examples of street artists creating 3D illusions on cement sidewalks. She will start with what she knows—charcoal, water color. Perhaps acrylic or oil.

The next day, because of the heat and crowds, Tessa opts on leaving Murphy in the rig for a few hours while she hikes down into the canyon. The campground has full hookups and they're in a good shady site. Murphy is safe and, after their morning run, he seems more than willing to stay in the coolness of the air conditioning in the rig.

The rangers forewarn everyone that for whatever distance anyone hikes down, it will be twice as much to hike up. They advise taking twice as much water than what you think you need. Some people heading down double back right away, saying, "We need more water."

Mr. Forsythe's instructions do not expect her to make it to the Colorado River.

"The Grand Canyon is built on erosion. Go as far as you wish down the trail. Anywhere along the way is acceptable."

Many people, in varying stages of fitness, are attempting the trail. Young boy and girl scouts and foreigners are clattering away, the kids laughing and teasing and running as fast as they can down. Others are trudging back up the trail, looking winded and rationing whatever water they have left.

An older couple is seeking shade. A guided mule train is walking by, and hikers have to make way for the mules. Tessa sees the old couple struggling to stay out of the way, but looking shaky as they slowly proceed uphill. She maneuvers herself down to them and helps them find some rocks to sit on in the shade.

"Have one of my waters."

"Oh, we're almost to the top, aren't we?"

Tessa has only been on the trail fifteen minutes. Twenty tops. But these people don't look well. When she had taken the man's arm to help them to the shade, it was cold and clammy.

"It's okay, I brought four waters."

"Is your hair partly pink?" the older woman, now seated, asks, squinting.

Tessa nods and shifts where she is, so the woman doesn't have to look into the sun when she addresses her.

"On purpose?"

Tessa smiles.

The mules continue passing. Some of the riders are wearing really strong cologne and perfume.

"My, they stink, don't they?" the woman comments.

"The mules have to poop too," one of the last mule riders responds.

The old woman and Tessa giggle.

"I meant the perfume."

"I know, it gagged me too."

They act like teenagers together, and it provokes a grin from the woman's husband.

"Take my water," Tessa insists. "It's at least another forty-five minutes up."

"Thank you, angel."

Tessa holds both their hands a moment before moving on. She follows a safe distance behind the mule train. She turns back and her eyes see a shimmering as these two become younger people now, their heads bent together, laughing lightheartedly with each other, as they remain on the coolness of the rock for just a few more moments.

AUNT SADIE'S JOURNALS are opening Tessa's eyes to another dimension of the places she's visiting. Sometimes, in a crowd, she'll see the back of a woman's head, her hair in ringlets, like a young Sadie.

When she's driving in the Ford, her hands gripping the steering wheel with the black leather padding wound around it, she can almost imagine looking over and seeing Sadie laugh at some remark from Percy.

Sometimes in the evenings, when she's walking Murphy around a sparsely filled campground, they'll come upon two couples laughing and roasting marshmallows, and that shimmering thing occurs. Tessa will recall a photograph of her aunt and uncle with another couple from the road.

In some ways, when Tessa is down by a body of water, it's like Uncle Percy and Aunt Sadie are right behind her. Maybe that's why she senses she's being followed. Maybe it's not creepy Uncle Chuck at all. Maybe it's her ancestors.

CHAPTER 16

AT ZION, TESSA scores a campsite right next to the Virgin River. It is roaring. A series of recent heavy rains have engorged the river and she can hardly hear herself think as she relaxes in the outdoor chair.

She and Murphy are in the shade of a grove of short, but old trees. Tessa hasn't been sleeping very well, waking in the middle of the night, disoriented and not knowing where she is.

Murphy's tail thumps beside her when she sits up, as if he is saying, *"I'm still here."*

Tessa wonders what's nagging at her, a sense of foreboding, or is she still looking over her shoulder for Uncle Chuck? She has some sense that she's being followed, but when she looks and looks hard, she sees nothing.

She attempts to paint the picture she took of the Grand Canyon. Focusing on her heart calms her. A long pull-behind trailer, much newer than hers, parks at the site across the way. Six shrieking children hop out. They scurry for the play area. They are followed by two adult women, and then, six more children. It seems like a lot of people, even for that large of a trailer. The man driving the truck and a teenage boy in the passenger seat open their doors and begin unhooking their rig. The teenage boy with the cowboy hat takes one look at her and nods, and returns to his task.

Mormons.

"Howdy neighbor," a voice calls out above the Virgin River. A middle aged couple approach. "Noticed the Michigan tags. We're from Michigan and we're hosting a neighborhood bonfire tonight. Three sites to the left of you. Tan Motorhome. Bring your chair. We'll have s'more fixings."

"Thank you."

Tessa is so not going to a neighborhood s'more campfire. What does she have in common with these people?

That night, the troubled, upset, sensations prevent her from sleeping. She tosses and turns. Soon she's dragging her camp chair to the laughter three doors down. The circle is huge and all types of folks are sitting around it, including the Mormons and their teenage son and daughters. They enlarge the circle for her. The boy tries not to make eye contact, but his energy is focused on her. She catches him looking once or twice, but is involved in a conversation with Bill, the host.

"You play euchre, of course?"

She smiles. "I'm not competitive."

"Just for fun, just for fun. We have an informal card table for four. Us Midwesterners have to have a game or two?"

She agrees.

Before she knows it, all the other campers are grouped around trying to learn the game; the Benders are Island Pacific people, the Mormons, and the Hefrons from Rhode Island all watch as Tessa, Dianne, and Bill, and Jen, a twenty-something traveling from Columbus Ohio, all play.

Jen is good, and Tessa just plays off her lead. To end the game, Bill decides to play a loner, where he drops his partner with just two trump. Instead of winning a possible four points, he loses good-naturedly.

"What possessed you to try?" Tessa laughs.

Bill wiggles his eyebrows. "It's just for fun. Did you have fun that round?"

Tessa nods. "You're a risk taker."

"Oh, you bet he is." Dianne smiles.

"Have you hiked Angel's Landing yet?" Jen asks Tessa.

"No. I never heard of it."

"Awesome hike," the teenage Mormon boy says. He's standing directly behind Tessa, and his energy is buzzing into her. His hand is on the back of her card table chair. Just like with Paul. She turns and looks up at him, being careful not to show her cards to the others.

The boy smiles down at her. He may be her age, or a year younger. "It's high, but passable. The weather is supposed to be good tomorrow. There's chains and stuff, if you don't like heights."

"Chains?"

"Yeah. There's some sections that seem narrow and have drop offs on both sides, but it's easy." He shrugs.

"We hike it every time we come," his father adds.

"I'll go with you," Jen offers. "If you want to."

"Okay."

"Murphy might want to stay with us, for that one," Bill suggests.

"Really? You'd be all right with that? Because I don't want him to get hot."

"Yeah, it gets hot up top, that's for sure," the boy agrees.

As the fire dies down for the older folks, the kids decide to continue a campfire in an empty site on the edge of the campground, by some rocks and the river.

More young people from various sites join them and pretty soon it's a party. Everyone's dancing and laughing. Some are drinking beer, and some are hooking up and wandering off. The Mormon boy tries to engage her, but Tessa just keeps speaking with Jen. They talk about all their travels and where they've been and where they are going.

"I can make myself scarce if you need me to," Jen offers, nodding over to the young guy.

"Thanks. I'm not interested in hooking up with anyone. But don't let me slow you down."

Jen smiles. "I don't usually find someone else my own age traveling alone."

"Do you get a lot of shit on the road?"

"You mean, because I'm not white?"

Tessa nods.

"No, not really. Just like Bill and Dianne, people are pretty friendly. You get one or two idiots along the way, but they are the exception. Just trust your gut instinct. It really develops out here on the road. I'd say ninety-nine-point-nine percent of people are pretty awesome." Jen pauses. "I'm glad you want to go hiking tomorrow. It's always more fun with another person."

"Have you ever done Angel's Landing?"

"No, but I want to try. I like early starts, if that's okay with you. I don't like heat of the day hikes."

"Neither do I."

"Cool." Jen has deep dimples when she smiles, and Tessa relaxes in a safe space with her.

"Murphy is like the coolest dog ever." Jen is petting him as he lies sleeping between them. "I'm running to my rig for another beer, want one?"

Tessa shakes her head no.

"How about a water?"

"Okay."

As Tessa waits, she reflects that at both bonfires a blend of folks she might not normally hang with, like the Mormons, surprised her. Everyone striving to find common ground in conversation, hearty laughs of self-told mishaps on the road, enjoying new stories and histories together. She tells the one about her first dumping tanks mishap when the hose wasn't fitted into the dump station correctly and everything went flying everywhere. How helpful all the folks at the dump site were. Everyone around the campfire claim it has happened to them too. She feels they are just being nice, but it's good to laugh about it.

The music out of the old-fashioned boom box starts playing "Rock Around the Clock."

And she and Jen start dancing. Tessa is young and free, alive and alone, and yet, not lonely at all.

"I'M GLAD YOU still wanted to go hiking today."

Jen is leading up the well-worn switchback path. It's red and has rocks alongside. While steep at times it's not too bad. And just like the Mormon boy said, there are chains every now and then as they gain steeper access. Even for early in the morning, many people are on the trail. Most are going up; some have already been up and are jubilantly climbing down. Their faces a healthy blush and excitement that they "made it."

Curiosity propels Tessa and Jen higher.

A blend of folks here too, just like at the campfire. People from France, Germany, South America, Asians, First Nation. Just as Jen nods especially to other black people, Tessa nods to First Nation, and they grin and smile when they see her, sometimes arm bent at the elbow, a fist up in the air as a hello.

Lots of children attempt the climb, and a few elders who say, "I'm only going so far."

Some benches are spaced at intervals for folks needing to rest. Then they get to the top, or so they think and realize as they make the turn, there's actually a lot further to go.

Jen starts out on the ridge that has fifteen-hundred-feet drop offs on either side. Tessa starts and gets about thirty yards before she freezes. Although the ledge is wider than it looks, she can't do it. The drop offs on either side make her dizzy, and a little nauseous, like she's suspended in the clouds. Maybe on a different day this would be less threatening. Today she simply stops.

In the middle of the eight-foot wide and sometimes less wide ledge, is a chain the whole length of the mostly barren ridge line up through to the other side where there is vegetation again; a high path with trees. At the very end are people, stick people it looks like, standing on a wide open flat surface, overlooking the park, the highway, and the other high points of the mountains. Their little jubilant stick figures jump up and down and their happy shouts of achievement waft over to Tessa after a considerable delay. Then, there's a long drop arch to another, lower platform rock. Tessa is unsure if the trail ends there or up top; she can't see that far.

Tessa makes room for the others behind her, and once they pass, she moves off trail. Jen returns to where Tessa is sitting on a rock well beyond the path of other visitors.

"Are you okay?"

"I can't do it."

"It's okay. We don't have to."

"I don't want to hold you back. I can wait here." Tessa has tears in her eyes and hates her fear of heights. "I want to be able to do it."

"Well, let's just sit here. It's a good time to have water and a bite to eat."

They sit in silence and watch group after group come up and make the turn and keep going.

"Is it just me?"

"No, it's really scary, even though eight year olds are doing it."

Tessa laughs and shoves her.

Suddenly a family with two boys, about eight and eleven, make the turn. The younger boy sits down.

"Get up," the father tells the boy.

"I don't want to do it, Dad."

Tessa's heart twinges.

The dad pulls his son by the arm, standing him up. Others pass by as the mom and older boy wait. It's a constant parade of hikers willing to try the ridge.

"Man up, Garth. I'm not going to have you embarrassing this family."

Tessa flinches. It's all she can do to calmly stand and walk over and in a polite voice say, "He can stay here with us."

"No!" the father barely regards her. "He is going to learn to face his fears, whether he likes it or not. I'm a primary electric lineman. I climb poles all day. He's going to learn how to do this."

"Let him be." The words erupt from her belly.

Jen is beside her in a flash. "Easy there." She puts her arms around Tessa and pulls her back into her body.

The father looks around at Tessa and something in her eyes moves him backward a step. "I mean. I'm sorry. It's nice of you to offer, but he can't just not go."

"Why not?"

"Well, because we're going . . . as a family."

"It's not for everyone." Tessa's voice is still deep. She's almost growling.

She's re-living. Her fists are clenched. She's ready to take this man's head off.

For a moment everyone freezes. The mom and older brother are staring open mouth at her. The little boy is looking up hopefully toward her. The father is shrinking away, his face red, as if he is embarrassed, or, very frightened.

"C'mon, son," is all he says, and he marches the boy forward.

The boy whimpers and looks back at Tessa, with a plea in his eyes.

"I'll hold onto you," the father says, a little more kindly.

"Let's go this way." Jen guides Tessa to their shady spot and they sit back on the rock. "Man. Now I know what it means to see a person's eyes turn yellow. Girl, you transformed. That guy was scared of you. Everyone was scared of you. That's some deep shit."

"It's not right, making that boy go when it's obvious he didn't want to. That's fucking abuse. I'm sorry." Tessa puts her head down. "It's just wrong. I don't know where that all came from."

"You went somewhere else."

Tessa nods.

"You've got power. Just another thing I'm attracted to."

They sit in silence a moment.

Last night, at the fire, Jen had leaned in for a kiss and it felt good. It felt more than good. They kissed for what seemed like hours, but Tessa couldn't go any further. Despite her raging hormones, she kept seeing Dina's face.

"That girl better know how lucky she is," Jen says, referring to Dina.

"Oh, you like the growly Tessa?"

Jen laughs. "Oh yes, ma'am. I would love me some of that growly Tessa."

They nudge shoulders.

"Let's go up this way." Jen indicates away from Angel's Landing. "We can get just as high, if not higher, and you can take a picture, paint it, and send it to me sometime, yes?"

"Yes," Tessa agrees.

As they stand, she places her hand on Jen's forearm. Electricity jumps between them and for a moment they both just stay still.

"Thank you. For everything. For being sane back there when I wasn't."

"My pleasure. If nothing else, I'm a good foxhole friend. I've got your back."

"And I've got yours."

"You can whoop ass too. I see that."

They high five and climb higher than Angel's Landing.

THE AHRENS HOST another campfire with a rousing game of euchre. Tessa begs off early so she can hook her truck and rig for her departure the next day. No sooner is she asleep than a loud knocking on the camper begins.

"Park Ranger! Everyone must evacuate in fifteen minutes. The dam has broken. The river is going to flood the campgrounds."

Tessa jumps to her feet. In a matter of minutes, she moves along with all the other campers. Lights on, engines running. People picking up camp. After Tessa throws her camp chairs in and gets Murphy in the truck, the awning up and the stairs stowed, she checks on the Ahrens and her other neighbors. Everyone is moving forward skillfully.

The vehicles follow each other like a well-organized parade. Up up up the highway they go and eventually they all begin turning, where a regular person, a camper, stands with a flashlight, waving them in. This side road also goes up a steep grade. A woman with a flashlight, no park ranger, is guiding people in. Once the vehicles enter a large area, other campers are helping vehicles park. When her rig is situated safely, Tessa sees if she can help. She guides vehicles of all shapes and sizes, illuminating their path, with her lantern. She reminds herself of an old railroad guide, swinging the bright LED lantern so drivers can see the way clearly.

"Stack 'em in as close as possible so we can fit as many as we can. We'll sort it out in the morning," calls one of the other guides. Tessa raises her light in acknowledgement and parks each one as close as she can and as organized.

Soon, everyone has been moved to higher ground and in short order, engines switch off, lights go out, and an eerie silence overtakes a hundred rigs parked in the high desert.

The next morning, Tessa works her courage up. After seeing Angel's Landing, she decides the rooftop of her rig is not that high. She climbs up, still tenuous, but manages to take a picture. She is one of the first ones awake. As she climbs down, Bill Ahren is there with a cup of coffee for her.

"Why, howdy do, young lady."

"Hi. And thank you."

"Fine morning."

"Yes, it is."

"You know," he waves his coffee cup at the sight before them, all the rigs parked in orderly fashion, everyone safe, "this is why I don't believe all the doomsday people, the politicians, The Corporate Run Nation that we are becoming. Ordinary people do extraordinary things. In crisis, the best of people come out."

"It's awesome how everyone worked together. I didn't see any official people last night."

"Nope. One experienced soul led us to higher ground and once we were all here, we helped each other fit in. Yep. It's a fine morning indeed."

He strolls back to his rig.

Tessa takes in yet another lesson and friends from the road.

CHAPTER 17

THREE DAYS BEFORE she's to meet Dina, their evening FaceTime call comes in. Tessa frowns. It's a regular call.

"No FaceTime? "

"Oh, baby, I couldn't bear to look at your face."

"What's wrong?" Acid pours into Tessa's stomach.

"I was really trying to avoid this . . ."

"What is it?"

"I have to postpone our plans . . . but just for a week. Good thing I got flight insurance."

"I don't understand."

"Oh, sweetie. I wish I could reach right through the phone right now. I can feel your disappointment. No one is more disappointed than I."

I doubt that.

"JR broke her leg playing coed softball. The lead professor of the cyclotron asked me to come in and babysit the last reports. This could be a real step up for me."

Tessa is speechless.

"Johnson is out because he got caught shooting meth. Can you believe that dickweed? Totally blew his scholarship for next year. Handed everything on a silver platter and he upends it. Fucktard. And Muriel Jubb is out because she decided to go to that seminar in Pittsburgh, which leaves me. I'm totally on for this. Baby? Are you there?"

Tessa nods, realizes what she's doing and clears her throat. "Yes."

"I'm soooo sorry, but really, it's just a week. JR can crutch it in after that. If it wasn't so important I would never do this in a million years. I took all the measures so it won't mess up your timing too. I rerouted myself through Seattle. We have two whole weeks together. It'll be awesome. Okay?"

"Okay."

"You're not saying very much. That means you're mad at me."

"I'm not mad at you," Tessa lies.

"Okay. You're mad at the situation."

"I'm disappointed."

"Oh, I know. Me too. But I promise, I'll be there in Seattle. One week and three days. Baby? I've gotta go. It's three hours later here and I am beat."

"Okay."

"I love you, Tessa."

"I love you more."

She can see Dina smiling all the way from Michigan.

"Bye for now, punkin. Sweet dreams."

THE NEXT TIME Dina FaceTimes her Tessa doesn't answer. She lets the little ringtones on the iPhone go on and on. Fifteen minutes later, Dina tries again. Tessa looks at the time on the phone. Ten p.m. here, one a.m. Michigan. She lets it go again. The phone doesn't ring again. She suffers a little guilt, because she knows she's being petty, but something won't let her pick up.

She continues watching *Fried Green Tomatoes*, one of the DVD's she found under the bed in the storage compartment. It's the good part, in the restaurant, as Idgie is saying, "Believe me when I say, I'm as settled as I ever hope to be . . ."

After the FaceTime goes unanswered, Tessa waffles about calling back and instead shuts off the phone.

SINCE DINA IS not flying into San Francisco, Tessa changes her route so she can see part of Yosemite. She decides to touch the southern edge and takes a hike up to a stand of ancient sequoias.

Here too, pictures she's seen in books do no justice to these otherworldly trees. Their sheer size and age, their space and intense presence is palatable for her, overwhelming her. A deep sacredness permeates this ground. How can people even think of cutting these beings?

Some of the sequoias have large open areas at the trunk. She touches the bark with both her palms. If she relaxes she senses a low vibration under the bark. From this stand of sequoias, she can overlook a huge valley. She snaps a picture of the valley. Then she snaps a picture of the first sequoia she met. It seems to beckon her.

It isn't on the agenda, but Tessa is moved to leave a little bit of Aunt Sadie inside the trunk of this sequoia. She believes her aunt doesn't mind at all.

She's grateful she can walk pain free. She sees so many others struggling with limps or packs or weight. Her young legs and lungs carry her into the higher atmosphere and she remembers. She's supposed to call Paul before she goes into the Canadian Rockies. Something about adjusting the carburetor and timing for the higher altitude of the Rockies. She could have a garage do it. But something inside her wants to be independent, free, and Paul said he'd guide her through it.

Paul answers her FaceTime right away. "Your hair is getting long."

"Think so?" she turns her head side to side. She's flirting lightly and they both grin.

"So what's the best thing you've seen so far?"

"Well, the Grand Canyon is definitely awesome, but so are the Gila Cliff Dwellings, and even the City of Rocks."

"City of Rocks?"

"It's a primitive campground way out in the middle of the desert. It's about thirty miles from the Mexico border."

"Dangerous? Drug runners?"

"Nooooooo. It's all desert, and then from nowhere these huge monolithic rocks spring up. The sunsets are amazing there. And the stars at night? Brilliant. I didn't know there were so many stars in the sky. The sequoias at the edge of Yosemite are spectacular. They are like people to me."

"How so?"

She smiles because Paul is seriously listening to her.

"Because, when I stand near them, they emanate. They're like people giant trees, breathing, moving, like they could almost walk."

"Wow. One of these days . . ."

"You're going to get out of that garage and travel."

"Yes! Now, tell me about the truck? How has it been running?"

"Perfectly. Do I need an oil change soon?"

"Truthfully? You can go five thousand miles; you'll be all right."

"How about the Canadian Rockies?"

"How far are you from there?"

"About a week. Maybe ten days."

"Okay. Call me once you're over the border, before you get on any twelve percent grades. It won't cost more will it? From Canada?"

"Mr. Forsythe took care of all that. He arranged with the phone service."

"Cool, dude. So . . ." Paul's green eyes look directly at her. "Miss me?"

Tessa hesitates.

"Oh, I know, your heart belongs to someone else, but just for a moment let me pretend. Close your eyes and tell me."

Tessa closes her eyes. She does like Paul. There's something about him that intrigues her. She opens her mouth and closes it.

"What?" he asks.

"Is this like I'm imagining for the rest of my life?"

"Imagine for more than just one night."

"Yes." She smiles, opening her eyes.

"Ha! I knew it."

"If you were a girl it would be better."

"Oh, man . . . that's just cold."

She overhears voices in the background, teasing him.

"Oh Paulllllllll!"

"Where are you?"

"Knock it off," he says to someone off screen. "Oh, just some douche at work." He turns again and says to the voice off camera more than Tessa, "He forgets I can fire his ass." He turns back to her. "Any problems on the road, I mean, with people?"

"Just Uncle Chuck." She hesitates.

"What?"

"Sometimes I feel someone is following me."

"Are they?" Paul asks sharply.

"No. I don't think so. Chuck creeped me out a little."

"You want me to break his legs?"

"No-ho, Silly."

"I could scare him."

"Then you'd be in jail, really? Do you want that?"

"No, but I'd tell him to quit fucking with you."

"You're sweet. I don't believe I've ever had someone offer to kick someone's ass for me. That's almost better than a date and chocolates."

"Now you're just messing with me."

She breaks into an open smile.

"Damn. Does it help if I say," Paul whispers, "that deep down I always wanted to be a lesbian?"

"Okay, that almost tops breaking someone's legs." She pauses. "You could have anyone you wanted. I'm just some sort of out of reach thing for you."

"It's not that. At all. And if you weren't in love, I would seriously date you."

"You're good for my ego."

"Yeah, well, mine's taking a beating. You said you fall for someone's eyes and their soul. Is that true?"

"Most of the time. The bond seems deepest with women."

"I like your eyes and your soul."

Tessa doesn't know what to say.

"Sorry," Paul apologizes.

"No, it's okay. I just don't know what to do with that."

"Just hear it, I guess."

"Paul?"

"Yes?"

"Be my friend. Keep being my friend."

He hesitates and then just says, "I will, Tessa. Bye."

"Bye."

TESSA MAKES HER way up the California coastline, and her next drop is near the border of Oregon in a place called Stout Grove. A different species of redwood from the sequoias grows in this ancient coastal redwood grove along the Smith River.

She and Murphy have the place to themselves. It's late afternoon as they walk and the sun slants into the mystical depths of the trees spiraling above them. Tessa imagines Jack and the Beanstalk, climbing into the heavens, into the canopy above where western songbirds nestle and sing. The winter wren being the loudest.

Here too, she is so small, surrounded by such giant living things, beings that have been around for upwards of two thousand years. What have they seen, felt, and lived? She tries to imagine the thousands of creatures that rely on them for their environment and living space through the centuries. She is having difficulty marrying her concept of time with these trees.

She finds the creek, lined with stones, leading to the river, and a great blue heron lifts off in front of them. A rock piper skitters along the shoreline, switching back and forth, looking for insects and prey under the various stones. Murphy wades into the creek water and his long back leg hairs waft with the current as the creek feeds into the larger, faster, river water.

Tessa crouches down and spills a bit of Aunt Sadie into the creek and watches the lighter ashes carry along the surface as they twirl and spin, turning into the stronger current.

The heavier ash, as always, sinks to the bottom.

She makes her way around the bend and sprinkles some more—the fast-moving current taking it downriver, the larger ashes disappearing into deep crevices.

How can no one else be here?

Tessa decides to camp and paint here for a few days, before moving north to her last mail drop, Florence, Oregon.

CHAPTER 18

THE JESSIE HONEYMAN State campground, even in late summer, has a lush tropical environment. She levels the rig, detaches, and drives north to the Siuslaw North Jetty.

Once they are on the vast expanse of beach, Tessa tosses the Frisbee for Murphy. The whole coastline in Oregon is public domain, protected from developers. It's as pristine as the redwoods; people taking care of their beaches.

Murphy is a natural Frisbee player. He leaps magically and twists and runs, fetching the Frisbee and dropping it at her feet before hightailing it down the wide beach for another throw. He sure doesn't act like an old dog.

Tessa spies a wall of sand with initials cut into it.

"PM and JM" in a heart shape. "FF / MG" and "SC loves PC."

Tessa stops dead in her tracks. What are the chances?

Sadie Cain loves Percy Cain. Tessa knows logically that these can't be Sadie and Percy's initials; it's just a coincidence. She wonders, out of the dozen initials scratched into this sand wall, how many are still together. How long can these initials possibly stand the wind or rising tide? Still some of them seem like they've been here more than a few days.

Below the sand initials in the wall is a fossilized Canada goose. Tessa inches closer and pokes it with a stick. Murphy pays no attention to it, trotting right by and finding a brush pile to urinate on. The fossilized goose is actually a piece of driftwood, perched like a bird reposing in the sand. It is hauntingly authentic.

As the sun sets, the wind whips in over the Pacific Ocean,

flapping at Tessa's hiking slacks and whipping Murphy's long fur.

"See you on the flip side!" Tessa calls. That night she paints the piece of driftwood and the initials wall. In her picture she adds, TW and DM. She can hope.

Tessa opens a journal from 1968.

> *Percy says that being with B and F makes him so alive. I am a little jealous, but aren't I the one that instigated all of this? Didn't I say, we should try? In the heat of the moment I was caught up by B's intelligence, her great smile. Do all couple's get restless, or is it just us?*

Whoa. Tessa flips forward a few pages, but no, there they are on summer vacation in Zion. She flips back near the front. Nothing about a B or an F there.

There is an entry that reads:

> *Percy says that a man has needs and it's his wife's duty to fulfill those needs. I asked him what archaic Neanderthal culture did he come from and this just proves men are two steps lower on the food chain; Einstein be damned! If they had let women into schools and hierarchy for the last few centuries we could be flying rockets and creating technology too. Oh we had it out we did. As much as I love him, some days I could just hate him. I swear. It's the little things that tell the big things about somebody. Sometimes he's just so self-absorbed. Either that, or his little head is doing all the talking for his big head.*

Yikes! Tessa does some quick math and discovers in 1968 was fourteen years into their marriage. She's a little ill that they weren't getting along. But they must have made it through. They were together till the end.

She finds more entries, some are happy, and some aren't.

> *Wasn't it bad enough we lost JFK in 1963? What are all these assassinations? Martin Luther King, Bobby Kennedy barely two months apart? Riots everywhere from Detroit to LA in 1967. This beloved country torn apart. And why, in God's name, are we still bringing home boys in body bags from Vietnam? God, these hawkish men and their war politics. B says we have an obligation to fight for women's rights. I agree with her. I've been fighting for women's rights since I was out of the womb!*

Tessa reads far into the night, but doesn't come across any references to who B or F are.

CHAPTER 19

"OH MY GOD! You're here."

Tessa has flowers from every destination they would have seen together if Dina had arrived in San Francisco. She has flowers from the river by Stout Grove, California, pinyon pinecones from New Mexico, wildflowers from Florence, Oregon, and many other little bluebells and tiny greens along the way.

Their hug is intense, and Dina kisses her neck. "I'm so glad to finally hold you."

She pushes Tessa back a little and looks into her eyes. "How are you? Anymore Uncle Chunk fiascos?"

"I'm okay. I've been waking up in the middle of the night, but then I fall asleep again."

"Your eyes do look tired. Once you show me how to drive the truck and camper, I can help there, if you want."

"Really?"

"Of course, baby."

They walk to the parking structure.

"Where's Murphy?" Dina asks.

"I left him in the camper. It's cool enough and we ran this morning. How about returning there and touring tomorrow? If that's okay with you?"

"Definitely. I'm beat. I could use a good stiff drink and put my feet up. Believe it or not, Dr. Lynch sent me with a couple of research items to finish. It won't take long. I can do them anytime along the trip, as long as there's Wi-Fi that shouldn't be too much of a problem. It's just huge he trusts me with it."

"I don't really have anything liquor wise, just a couple of beers in the fridge."

"No worries. We'll pass a store."

Tessa grins. "By the luck of the Gods I do have another treat you will enjoy."

Dina eyes widen. "Are you kidding me? You scored on the road?"

"Not exactly. I'll tell you on the way."

AT CAMP, AFTER formally hugging on Murphy and playing with him along the water, Dina pulls Tessa into the rig.

"Back to where we left off." Her eyes are bright and full of love.

Tessa teases her a little, standing off. "No drink? No putting your feet up? No writing a research paper for Dr. Lynch?"

Dina growls and grabs her. "Come here, you minx."

When Tessa wakes, she's alone in the rig and for a moment, she is totally disoriented. Did she dream being with Dina? Is she really still in Washington? Murphy's tail thumps on the floor as he hears her stir.

He pokes his head over the covers as he sits up and licks her hand.

"Tessa?"

Dina! It's not a dream.

Tessa throws the covers off and dresses hurriedly.

She scrambles outside.

No one's there.

"Yoo-hooo." Dina's voice comes from above her.

Tessa turns. Dina holds out her hand as she stands on the roof. "Come on up, the view is gorgeous."

With some trepidation, Tessa climbs onto the roof. Dina

had placed the rag rug on the new rubber roof and then considerately had put the two low camp chairs over the rug.

"You passed out, baby girl." Dina smiles.

"I guess I needed that." Tessa grins, despite her qualms of being on the roof.

Dina offers her a cocktail in a plastic martini glass. "For you. Only one drink per roof adventure."

They watch the sun begin its descent over Vancouver Island on the other side of the Straits of Juan de Fuca.

"How awesome is this, sweetheart?" Dina whispers. "I love you so much." She kisses Tessa on the cheek.

Tessa continues looking at the scenery, dropping her hand till it finds Dina's and clasping it.

"For a moment inside, I didn't know where I was. I was afraid I dreamt it all up, that you weren't really here."

"Baby, I'm sorry I was delayed, but I'm here now. I'm really, really here."

Tessa smiles. "You most certainly are."

AFTER DINNER, DINA offers to do dishes. She's done her part, keeping the rig clean, sweeping, keeping her items stowed neatly in one corner. Tessa believes that if they can cohabitate in less than two hundred square feet, anywhere else will be a breeze.

She suddenly realizes Dina is letting the water run in between rinsing the dishes. She comes up behind Dina and circles her arms around her.

"Baby?"

"Yes, love?"

"Thank you for doing the dishes, this is awesome." Then she reaches through and turns off the water. "I didn't explain that we don't have full hook ups here. Just the water and electric. So, when we run water, it fills the waste tanks."

It takes a moment for this information to register.

"I was doing them wrong." Dina is horrified.

"No, no no. You were doing them beautifully." Tessa turns Dina to face her. "Believe me, I had to learn all these things myself. I've screwed up so many times. One time the toilet almost swished up all over the floor."

"Ugh. Grotesque."

"No shit. Pun intended."

They laugh.

"And I don't put toilet paper in the tank. I have a wastebasket for paper."

Dina's eyes widen.

"TP messes with the gauges, hard to clean out."

"Geez T being in a rig is kind of barbaric. You have to watch every little thing."

"It does make us aware of how much electricity is used, if we're only on battery power, or using the solar panel. Rationing water, rationing waste."

"Forces us to have a smaller footprint, huh?"

"That's it."

"Did I over fill the tanks?"

"Well, let's see." Tessa shows Dina the light panel. "Nope, we're still fine till we pull out of here Tuesday. Then we'll dump the waste tanks, and make the rig as light as possible, except for good fresh water."

On Tuesday, Dina dutifully don's rubber gloves to help Tessa.

"You don't have to do this," Tessa says again.

"No. I want to." Dina has a stubborn streak that Tessa admires.

"Well, the first part is the worst. Best to try and be upwind."

Tessa shows Dina how to secure the sewer line at both ends so there's no snaky surprises, like what happened to her the first time.

She pulls the big valve and the sewage rushes out.

"Oh, yeah. I can see how that would spew all over."

"Now we rinse it out."

"With all that kitchen water I used. Let me do that part?"

Tessa steps aside.

Dina pulls the smaller drain handle. "Well, that's sort of cool."

"They have a water line here, just for cleaning."

After they've rinsed everything off and stowed it, Tessa pulls the rig ahead and makes one last check of the steps, the awning, and that the kayak is secure.

"You're a pro." Dina smiles. "Want me to take the first leg of the trip?"

"Maybe this afternoon?"

"Cool, I'll get me some big rig driving in. How far are we going today?"

"Well, I enjoy the state campgrounds and there's one just before we cross the border, near Wiser Lake. We can't cross with any contraband."

"Good point."

AT WISER LAKE, Dina and Tessa watch a kingfisher splash into the water and back out.

"This is so cool," Dina says. "We don't see anything like this at school, do we?"

Tessa shakes her head. "I wonder what the totem is of a kingfisher."

Dina punches on her iPhone. "It's a symbol of peace and prosperity. Very cool."

They smile, hugging their knees and watching until the day dips into evening.

TESSA IS SLEEPING in late, more than she likes. She's a different person with Dina, whose sexual appetite seems endless. Together their lovemaking is slow, delicious, charged with their friendship and love.

Dina is softly kissing her all around but nowhere near her most sensitive areas. Dina looks back and smiles, her hair is pulled up in a half twist and she slowly lowers herself to Tessa's mouth. Tessa breathes her in and softly begins kissing and Dina rises, just out of reach.

"No fair." Tessa growls and brings Dina's hips lower to her. Together they dance like this, teasing and licking, Dina's breasts intermittently brushing against Tessa's tummy—her hard nipples exciting Tessa. It's a dance, a duet, and sometimes a duel to see who will succumb first, give way and let the other take her. So far Dina has gotten her way every time.

And this time it's no different.

When Tessa climaxes, Dina gently moves a finger into her anus.

Tessa screams into a pillow, her mind, her soul are exploding to the stars.

It's several minutes before she's back in her body, on earth.

"How do you do that to me?"

By this time Dina has shifted and is enveloped in Tessa's arms.

"We do it together, love." Dina kisses her all about the face.

Tessa's heart is so full. If she dies right now, everything in her life is perfect.

"Your heart beat is so strong," Dina murmurs, her head resting on Tessa's chest.

"Mmmmmm." Tessa is determined to not fall asleep. She wants to be inside Dina, rocking her, kissing her, licking her, drinking her. She is in another time, another space, almost another world. When she sleeps, she sleeps hard and when she wakes, she is weightless and light, as if the sun could shine right through her.

Murphy is getting neglected. They haven't run in the last few days. Tessa slips out as quietly as possible, her running shoes in hand.

Murphy is beside himself. He is jumping up and down, literally grinning as Tessa slips on her running shoes. She gets them laced up and hears Dina's voice.

Tessa peeks her head in the camper.

"Where you going?" Dina's eyes are all squinty and her blond hair is mussed in about four different ways. She attempts to lift her head from the pillow.

"Just a quick run with Murphy, I'll be back soon."

"Mmmmm, come back to bed first."

"I will, I promise. Murphy needs to stretch his legs."

And so do I.

AS THEY PREPARE to cross the border, they each take tasks, to ready the rig and the paper work. Tessa slides into the driver's seat and instinctively checks the awning in her passenger side mirror.

"The sewer cap and the stairs," she says aloud, but to herself.

"I checked all that," Dina says from her open laptop.

But no, she didn't. From the circle mirror in the longer side view, Tessa can see the steps are out, and the levelling blocks are by the campfire.

"Sweet. I just need to check the bumper, make sure the end caps are on tight."

Tessa stows the stairs and the levelling blocks. Dina pokes her head out the window.

"Wow. My bad. I bet when that call came in from Dr. Lynch, I got distracted."

"That's okay," Tessa says. After all, she's used to doing this alone.

It's the little things that tell the big things.

Tessa looks behind her as if someone has spoken out loud, but no one is there.

At the border, Dina elbows her. "PLU."

Tessa is confused.

"People like us," Dina explains.

Still confused Tessa drives up to the border guard. It's a young woman. In uniform. Stern. Tessa attempts her best smile, handing over both their passports and Murphy's medical records.

"What's your destination?"

"Uhm, Kamloops highway."

The border guard gives her a withering glance.

"I mean we're camping along the way and then heading back home."

"Michigan? Both of you?"

"Yes."

"How long do you expect to be in Canada?"

"Two weeks?"

"Is that two weeks, or maybe more?"

"We have to be back by September first," Dina intervenes. She doesn't smile either. She's matching the border guard's energy, which doesn't go unnoticed.

The border guard surveys Dina coolly for an instant. "Any pepper spray? Automatic weapons? Pistols?"

Tessa shakes her head. "I have a shotgun though."

She hands over the registration for that.

The border guard sighs. "Pull over there for inspection."

She keeps their paper work.

They pull over for what seems like a very long time. Murphy is panting. Tessa opens her door to get his dog dish.

A voice over the PA says. "Stay in your vehicle."

"Don't be so nervous, T. They just like to intimidate people. Real butch. But she's totally doable."

Tessa looks at Dina horrified.

"What?" Dina laughs.

"You're incorrigible."

"I like looking at the menu."

The guard comes up. "Let's unlock your camper."

"Can I get my dog his water dish?"

"Yes."

The guard looks at Dina. "You can remain in your seat."

If Dina is tempted to reply, she shows no sign of it.

Tessa opens the camper and the guard, with another male guard, go inside. The female guard bends down and picks up Murphy's dish and hands it to Tessa.

"This is the shotgun case?" The other guard indicates the shotgun in the closet.

Tessa nods.

"Okay, you can go water your dog, but return here after."

"Wow," Tessa says to Dina as she pours Murphy water. "They sure are serious."

"They probably hate Americans."

"Technically they are Americans too."

"Yeah, well, US citizens."

"I have to go back."

"Lucky you." Dina already has her laptop open. "Hopefully they won't shoot me as I do my schoolwork."

Tessa returns to the camper.

"Okay, then. Everything checks out." The male guard leaves.

"Summer vacation?" the female guard asks.

Tessa nods.

"Well, enjoy Canada and don't speed." She never cracks a smile, but she does turn back and remarks, "Sweet truck."

Once Tessa is in the driver's seat, Dina watches the guard walk into the building.

"Oh, yeah, she's definitely doable. Nice ass."

Tessa shoves her.

"I tell you what, Tessa Williams. Loving you has popped my eyes wide open."

CHAPTER 20

"OH MY GOD, T. Is this what it's been like the whole trip?"

Dina is gripping the arm of the truck door while gaping at the entrance to the Canadian Rockies. They are approaching Revelstoke and Tessa's ash drop in the Columbia River. The cathedral of mountains and ice caps towers over them as they begin driving the majestic ranges.

"This is how the sequoias and redwoods felt."

"We have to come back. Two weeks is not enough. You can sense how ancient, stoic, and immovable they are."

Tessa is giddy with the sheer beauty of the area.

"Your great aunt and uncle sure knew how to sightsee."

"I bet the roads were a lot rougher back then. In fact, I know so. Sadie got so tired of changing tires. They carried at least two extra tires at all times. They had to take extra fuel too, 'cause gas stations were really far between."

"They were brave."

"Well, help always arrived when they needed it."

"I mean they didn't have cell phones or anything to call for help back then. If you got lost or stuck, you're on your own."

"Maybe that's why they would hook up with other couples and caravan together sometimes."

"That makes sense."

Part of Tessa wants to share all the secrets in the journals, but she is heeding Mr. Forsythe's words.

"So when do we call hunky mechanic guy?"

"Paul? Well, I thought after the ash drop. The grades haven't been too bad yet."

They take a road off the highway, west of Revelstoke. Tessa is confident she can find a place along the river and in a short distance she does.

"You don't have to come."

"You're kidding, right? Of course I want to come. But you might have to explain things to me."

Dina watches her ritual intently, quietly standing back as Tessa thinks about Percy and Sadie. She's unsure what year they were here, but it seems later than the trips out west. Were they happy on this trip? Or is this when Sadie thought Percy was two steps lower on the food chain? Maybe the photo albums will have pictures with locations and dates.

When she finishes, Dina comes up and hugs her, full bodied.

"That was awesome, T. It's really special what you're doing."

"And this leg of it is almost done. Let's head over to the campgrounds and get set up."

"Okay. Will it be too late to call . . . ?"

"Paul?"

"Paul."

"No, I don't think so."

DINA'S INSIDE, BEGINNING dinner prep, so Tessa makes the call.

"Hey. You're in Canada now, eh?" His dimples accentuate his wide grin.

"Funny."

Dina springs out of the rig with a dishtowel in her hand. Her blond hair is done up in a French twist and she has her short shorts on.

"Hi, Paul. I'm Dina." She's wiping her hands. "Just got all the veggies cut for the kabobs." She puts one hand on Tessa's shoulder.

"Oh. Hi, Dina."

Paul looks at Tessa as if he got caught in the headlights.

"Uhm, Dina? Could you give Murphy a walk? I think he needs to pee."

"Sure. Be back in a jiffy. Nice to meet you Paul." Dina leans in again and waves to the iPhone.

"Sorry 'bout that," Tessa says when Dina is out of hearing.

Paul swallows hard. "It would be so much better if she had a mole on her nose or three heads. She's absolutely stunning. Who can compete with that?"

Tessa looks down.

"It's okay, Tessa. I'm glad you called me. Now let's adjust the carburetor, okay?"

"Okay."

Paul explains the simple procedure of allowing the carburetor more air. "Once you get below a certain altitude, you have to do that in reverse, or it's going to run shitty, okay?"

"Okay."

"Okay. Cool. If you can, test it out without the camper on it, make sure everything is running smoothly. Any problems, call me back. You remember how to adjust the timing, right?"

"Loosen the bolt on the distributor and turn the cap slowly, if the truck is running rough."

"Right. If all else fails, you have that one city you'll be hitting . . ."

"Canmore."

"Yeah, they have a shop there. They can adjust the timing and the carb for you if you want them to do it."

"Thanks, I really appreciate it."

"No worries. You take care."

Dina returns with a grin. "Green eyes. He is kind of hunky."

"He's sweet. A good friend."

"Well, we can't have too many friends, that's for sure."

As they enter the rig, Dina shows Tessa her handiwork with the skewers of veggies she's made up. "So, I was just going to add some seasonings . . ."

Dina picks up the Cajun spices bottle.

"Uhm, honey?"

"Yeah, baby?"

Tessa grabs Dina's hand before she sprinkles Aunt Sadie on their food. "Whoa, I put some of Aunt Sadie in here."

Dina's eyes widen in horror. "But whatever for?"

"Cousin Joe, his girlfriend . . ."

"Oh, wow. Totally forgot that story. Freaky."

"But everything else is exactly what it says it is."

THE CLIMB OVER the Rockies is thrilling and nerve-racking. Tessa takes the steep grades carefully, seeing other vehicles towing rigs, stopped off to the side, steam coming from their engines. Some are struggling up the grade with black smoke coming out the exhaust. Fuel. She keeps an eye on her gauges and has shifted the truck in to second. Midnight Rider climbs Highway 1a like a champ. She is having a hard time keeping her eyes on the road while attempting to catch glimpses amid the towering beauty as the mountain ranges become more dramatic and vertical.

Dina is oohing and ahhing out the window. For once, the laptop is gone, out of sight, and she is just enjoying the moment. As they descend into the Canmore area, Tessa keeps the rig in second to spare the brakes, once the grade is not so steep she shifts up into drive.

"You're a pro, baby. I'm glad you did that part of the driving. Have you ever seen anything more beautiful in your life?"

"No. Never. My mom would love this."

"Mine too, but I can't ever see me doing a trip like this with her."

"Too much alike?"

"Oh, I'd just do everything wrong. Never good enough."

Tessa wants to ask her more, but Dina excitedly points out the bridge overhead.

"Check it out, Tessa. A wildlife crossover bridge. It's made just for the animals."

As Tessa approaches the land bridge, she sees a natural corridor with trees and shrubs. High fencing on either side keep the wildlife as safe as possible.

"I've always heard of those, how cool to actually see one," Dina says. "They must put 'em where there's already a trail, right?"

"You'd think so."

"So where are we stopping today?"

"It's not too far up. Hopefully we can get in. It has over three hundred RV sites."

The Provincial Park is busy. Campers of all shapes and sizes are parked in very neat and widely spaced grounds. Tessa follows the directions to the very last row of sites. Each row is higher than the last one, terraced upwards, and when they park, Tessa sees why.

Across a wide valley and soaring up into the sky is a huge snow-capped peak, high on the left side and a sharp descent to the right. Although plenty of daylight is left, it's technically evening, and a bright planet is juxtaposed a few degrees up and off the left of the mountain peak.

They both stare at it openmouthed.

"Is this heaven?" Dina breaks the silence.

Murphy wants out. It's been a long day for him, and Dina solicitously takes him for his walk. Five minutes later she is back wide-eyed and speechless. She just points to the service road behind them.

It's up a rise too.

"Wha?" Tessa laughs.

Dina opens her mouth, says nothing, and shakes her head.

Murphy is staring intently uphill.

"What is it?"

"B-B-B-bear."

"What?"

"Well, it ran away as soon as it saw us, but it was scratching a tree up pretty good."

"You're not in East Lansing anymore."

"That's for sure. I think Murphy and I are going to walk downhill, through the campground."

"Are you okay?"

"Seriously, yeah. I just have to understand how much wildlife there actually is around here."

Later, as they are doing dishes, they get another reminder. Something bumps on the trailer, and Murphy pricks up his ears and cocks his head.

Tessa looks out the camper window. A very large, female elk is nonchalantly licking out of Murphy's water dish beside the step. Every time she steps side to side she nudges the rig. And when her side hits the rig, she very considerately moves away. Dina squeals and takes movies with Tessa's iPhone.

"They're protected here, did you know that? Awesome. I can't think of a better honeymoon."

Tessa's heart bursts wide open with joy.

AS THE LATER evening comes on, the dusky, not quite dark blue evening hue, they sit outside and watch the female elk. She has moved down the way to an unoccupied pop-up. The people left their garbage tied to the handle of the door. The animal has gently peeled away an opening and is nibbling on whatever she can pick out of the contents.

"Should we do something?"

Tessa considers this for a moment. "Nah. She looks like she's done this all before and she is being very gentle."

"How late do you think it is?"

It's a game. Ever since being further north, the daylight has gotten much longer.

Tessa gives it her best guess. "Ten?"

"Nope. Almost eleven."

They shake their heads and look at the planet near the mountain.

Dina holds up her phone and selects a night sky app.

"Venus. Of course it's Venus." Dina kisses her and doesn't stop kissing her even once they're inside the rig.

IN THE MIDDLE of the night, Tessa is shaken awake by Dina.

"You're having wormhole nightmares again."

Tessa rolls over and looks at her questioningly.

"You drop through the rabbit hole to somewhere else. It's actually kind of scary. You stop breathing."

"I do?"

"You talk about worms and mud and whimper, 'Stop!' and 'It hurts!' Then you quit breathing."

Dina snugs her into her shoulder.

Tessa is astounded. "Why would I be having nightmares?"

"I dunno, baby, but it's all alright. I'm here now."

One of the nightmares Tessa actually remembers. She even wakes herself from it before Dina does.

She's ten years old. They're at Uncle Chuck's house in Westland, near Detroit. She hates going there as much as her dad does. But it's a big birthday party for Uncle Chuck. Tessa takes off with Cousin Joe and one of his friends. They hike back to a swamp with big old growth and long dark veiny grape vines hanging down. She's brought her fiberglass long bow. It's lime green. And she has new arrows, not sharp like deer arrows, just the blunt ones.

The bull frogs are huge and Joe takes a swipe at a couple with his arrows, losing both immediately. The other kid hits one and misses another. Tessa takes aim and shoots one clean through, then another. Pretty soon all three kids are shooting and laughing and goading each other on until it's a complete massacre.

Suddenly Tessa stops, sickened to her stomach. She's just grabbed the shaft of her arrow from a very large frog, impaled straight through the gut. Its white belly floats up to her and the lifeless legs and body of this particular frog sears its memory into her brain. The perfectly round hole with blood at its edges stares back at her like a lifeless eye of God. She freezes.

The boys are still shouting and laughing and splashing through the pond, trying to kill more frogs.

Tessa looks at all the bodies floating upwards, dead. Mostly because of her. Because she's such a good shot.

She turns and runs. She runs with the bow in one hand and the bloody arrow in the other, and her pack of quills in her holder on her back. She runs through the meadows, letting the grasses slap her face and bare thighs, running up and down wheel ruts heavy equipment left behind. She hears Joe calling for her and she runs blindly, crying and sickened, suffocated. She doesn't stop till she reaches the edge of Uncle Chuck's back yard and then she slows and sinks into the grass so she's completely hidden.

She tries to wipe the blood off the arrow and she takes the sheath off her back. She holds her bow and regards it for a moment. She loves this bow. But she doesn't love what she's just done. Her legs are full of bog mud and slime and all she can see for months after, in her dreams, are the white bellies of frogs floating up to meet her.

Slowly she lurches upwards. She staggers to her father's car. She stows her bow and arrows. She never touches them again.

It's the memory of the white bellies of the frogs that wakes Tessa up now. She holds the blanket up to her neck and looks to see if she's wakened Dina. Dina's soft snores and poofing breaths indicate she's still sleeping.

Although it's a warm night, Tessa's teeth are chattering.

Murphy comes to the side of the bed and lays his head beside her. She inches her arm out and pets him. How does he know she is crying?

She'd swore an oath that day of the frogs. Never again would she take another life unless she absolutely had to. Never again would she harm another animal or human if she could help it.

She knows she needs to make reparations for all the frogs she killed and one day, it will be clear how she needs to do it. For now, all she can do is promise.

Troubled, she finally turns on her side and circles Dina's waist. Dina makes a small sound, as if partially waking, and shifts enough so Tessa can burrow her head into Dina's back. She wonders why the memory comes now. What lesson about her part of massacring the frogs does she need to heed?

It's a long time before she sleeps, and when she does, she remembers Murphy and his constant energy protecting her.

CHAPTER 21

THE HIKES THEY take the next three days are long ones. They pack for the day, taking almond butter and homemade jam purchased from roadside stands and packing Murphy with extra drinking water and his doggie treats. They wear whistles in case they come upon bear and eagerly scamper over rocks and streams to find glaciers off road.

Murphy leads them down the trail alongside a loud rushing creek. No one else is hiking this trail and it's an easy incline with a high ridge to their right. Tessa is moved to crouch beside the icy cold creek. She cups the water in her hands and drinks.

"Oh my god, Tessa." Dina is standing over her. "You could get giardia or something."

Where does all of Dina's fear come from? Tessa is mystified. She stands, smiles, and French kisses Dina right there.

"Wow!" Dina drops down and tastes the water too.

Murphy has stopped several yards ahead of them and laps from the glacial torrent.

All of a sudden, above the thundering creek, the roar of a surprised bear resounds in their ears.

"Blow that damned thing," Tessa tells Dina.

Murphy hears neither the bear nor the whistle over the sound of the creek; he is busily sniffing a bush to the side of the trail and lifting his leg.

"Do we go on?"

Tessa listens. "I think that bear has moved on. Sounds like she was startled to even see other life."

They choose to hike toward the glacial lake. A half hour later, they remove their boots and cool their toes in emerald glacial waters. Murphy dips almost his whole face into the water, attempting to retrieve a lodged stick. He paws at it and tries again.

"It's our own private paradise."

"This happens all the time," Tessa agrees. "Most people quit hiking after a couple of miles."

"I don't get it."

"Well, some can't."

"But the others? Why don't they choose to . . . ?"

"Time?"

"I've only been traveling with you a little while, but time seems like a foreign concept to me now. And, I'm glad it is."

So am I.

THEIR FIRST DAYS together are something out of a movie. They are in love and in bliss. They make love day and night. They make love outside on their hikes with Murphy on watch and seemingly unruffled . . . Everything is perfect. Except Murphy's eating is erratic.

Tessa offers him burger with his kibble. He sniffs it casually and walks over to the couch. Dina has her nose in her laptop.

"He's not eating."

"Well, maybe it's the daylight thing. You know it's crazy there's only four hours of night. That's throwing me off. I feel manic."

"Yeah, but he should be eating more not less."

"I dunno."

Tessa looks up and sees Dina is back into her laptop, the "I dunno" an almost dismissal of the problem.

Tessa holds her hand over his nose. It's wet and cool,

normal. Murphy wags his tail and rolls over on his back, offering his belly. In all other ways, he seems normal. He's not puking.

Dina gets up and makes herself another drink.

"Why do you drink every night?" Tessa asks.

Dina measures out some vodka and turns from the counter. "Oh, I don't know. Vacation?" She hands Tessa a glass.

Tessa sniffs it.

"It's a very good vodka. Very smooth. Go ahead, try it."

Much later, Tessa pours out the rest of her vodka, hoping Dina doesn't notice, but she does.

"Oh, honey, don't feel like you've got to drink because I do. But next time, let's just pour it back in the bottle okay? By the way, I have an assignment ready to send, but there's no Wi-Fi here, what are the chances of getting to a location that has some?"

"Our chances tomorrow are excellent."

"Tonight's probably out of the question?"

Tessa reviews the distance. "It would be better tomorrow. If you can wait."

Dina sighs and shuts the laptop. "I wish that referral from Dr. Houseworth would come in. She'll make all the difference of me getting accepted for grad school."

Dina sits next to Tessa and Murphy on the floor.

Tessa combs Dina's long blond hair with her fingers. "You're getting in. I know it."

"Thanks, love, but I get a little nerved up waiting. There's just so much riding on it. When do you think you'll return to school?"

"Probably after this trip."

"Well, you'll get into grad school two years after me; then I'll be heading for my doctorate. Staggering our post-grad degrees is a really good thing; we won't be both under pressure at the same time."

Tessa is uneasy at even the mention of school or graduation. Sometimes the whole process of post-grad degrees seems more of a hazing, depending on what degree is being sought. How many times had she heard universities were just a business, cramming unneeded courses into a higher degree? How many conversations at the Union had she overheard of grad and doctoral students one upping each other with inevitable stories of favoritism, and how banal undergrads were? As if, a mere semester ago, they weren't the ones being taught by self-aggrandizing peers?

No. If Tessa is going to pursue another degree it might be an MFA. On the other hand, if a degree existed for traveling . . .

"Where are you, baby?"

"Thinking about school."

"My bad." Dina unties the red headband holding Tessa's long brown locks and then kisses her. And all thoughts of that other world slip away.

TESSA IS SO focused on getting Dina Wi-Fi she misses the North Saskatchewan River ash drop.

"Shit! Shit!" Tessa says. "I've never missed an ash drop."

"Oh it's okay, baby. Just dump the ashes at the next river crossing and take a picture and call it good."

"I can't do that."

"Why not?"

"'Cause this is a sacred thing. It's important. You said yourself it was."

"I know I did. And it is sacred. But, it's not a job. Who's going to know?"

"I'm going to know."

"Well, why is it so important if it's at that exact location? You've had to pass up other drops. You said Mr. Forsythe was cool about it. Wouldn't he understand not back tracking two hours?"

"I don't know."

Tessa is upset and angry and she's unsure why. All she knows is, she needs to return to make it right. She recalls it has to do with the river flowing into a specific ocean. She'd have to re-read Mr. Forsythe's instructions, but she doesn't want to do it now, in front of Dina. She'll just have to unhitch and take the truck back up the highway sometime. Maybe when Dina is sleeping, or writing e-mails on her laptop.

Now they have to make camp. Even though it seems bright daylight, it is getting toward eight p.m. and Tessa wants to make camp and settle in.

She hasn't run in a couple of days; she knows this always lifts her mood. Tomorrow, for sure, she's running, no matter how rewarding Dina makes staying in bed feel.

Tessa wakes with the dawn. She loves the sunrises. She stretches, slips on her shorts.

"But I like when you bring me coffee in bed first." Dina says, turned on her side.

Tessa looks up. "If I bring you coffee in bed, then we make love and I never run."

"Is that all bad?" Dina smiles. "Don't I give you a work out?"

"Oh, yes. It's an awesome workout."

"Let's put a Fit Bit on you and see how many calories you're burning."

Tessa leans over. She kisses Dina on the forehead. "Sweetie, I'll be back in no time, promise. Murphy and I need to do this."

"You have more of a relationship with that dog than you do with anyone else."

"That's not fair. He's been with me the whole time."

"It's just a joke, T."

It upsets Tessa that Dina is calling her by a letter. She's unsure why, but she doesn't like the tone of it.

After lunch, they hike Athabasca Falls.

Tessa chooses to perform the ceremony, dispersing the ashes away from the hordes of people.

She looks up to see an old man with a quirky smile watching them. Usually this would creep her out, but something about this person is soft and kind.

"A grandmother?" he asks.

"Great Aunt."

"Ahhh." He nods. His walking stick looks uniquely carved.

"Is that your work?"

He smiles.

"It's beautiful."

Unspoken, they begin walking together. Dina is further ahead with Murphy. She's out of hearing, picking up rocks one at a time, perusing their individuality and just as quickly dropping them.

"It's a great testament for the young to honor the old."

"Aunt Sadie is still teaching me. Especially on this trip."

He stops and looks at the river. "Have you ever shared solitude? For example, saying nothing, doing nothing for hours, over a campfire? When that sort of intimacy is shared with just one other person, it can be the most profound intimacy of all."

Tessa smiles.

"It is kind of you to share with an elder." He nods toward Dina and Murphy. "They wait for you."

Tessa reaches Dina and senses she's out of sorts. "What is it?"

"I don't know." Dina keeps looking at the rock she's just picked up, Murphy's leash in her hand. "There's just something about you. People are drawn to you. Strangers. They just come up and start talking to you."

"Does it bother you?"

Dina looks up at the mountains. She can't, or won't, look Tessa in the eyes.

"I don't know. I just don't get it. I don't know what I'm feeling. It's silly to say jealous. I mean, I have things I want to speak with you about, but then, it's like these strangers have more importance than I do."

"It's not that."

"I feel stupid for even saying anything."

"You can't help what you're feeling. I want to know. I can tell when something is off."

"That's just it. You're such an empath. It's just uncanny."

Dina finally looks at her, the cute pucker between her brows. "It's those damn penetrating dark brown eyes you have. People just get swallowed up in them, don't they?"

Tessa has no words.

"How can I blame them?" Dina kisses her.

CHAPTER 22

DINA IS ON the laptop doing research, shuffling e-mails about school and grad school, getting references, talking with big wigs all over the world.

"Have a nice jog, baby?" Dina finally looks up from her laptop.

"It's gorgeous . . . come share?" Tessa grabs the urn to divvy some ashes outside for the Saskatchewan ash drop.

"You bet. I was just buttoning this up annnnnnnnnnd . . . I have a surprise for you." Dina waves a piece of paper. "I signed us up for an overnight horseback riding adventure. We might get a chance to see white wolves."

"Seriously?"

"Yeah. I spoke with the tour guide specialist and he recommended this as the absolute best time. My only wish is we could have gone for the whole week. They have gourmet meals and set up our lodging and everything."

"Come outside."

"Okay."

Tessa reads the flyer. "We can't go on the ride."

"Why not?"

"Murphy can't go."

"Well, that's kind of the idea, the white wolves won't come around a dog, I don't think."

"But he's never been boarded. I'm unsure how it will affect him."

"Geez, T, it's only one night. Probably not even an entire twenty-four hours. He's just a dog."

"He's not just a dog to me."

"That's a bit harsh. You're going to blow a one-in-a-million chance to see white wolves because the dog can't go? It's not rational."

Dina's hands fly out. They hit Tessa's arm. By design or mishap, the open urn goes flying.

"Oh my god." Tessa is on the ground trying to gather the ashes up. Some are already mixing in with the soil. Frantically picking through the grass and sawdust chips, her heart is pounding and she's near tears. She manages to gather half of what's left.

"I'm sorry, Tessa." At least Dina is trying to help gather the ashes. "We got the largest portion of it, I think. I'm so sorry. I'm so clumsy sometimes."

"It's okay. I know you didn't mean to do it."

"I guess I'm just upset we can't go. I had planned this surprise for us, as a special gift. Just you and me."

"I know, and it's an awesome idea. But we can do it next time? If Murphy was eating a little more and not just eating grass and making himself puke, I would consider it."

"Maybe it's time to take him to the vet?"

"Maybe." Tessa looks down at him.

He looks up and wags his tail. His eyes are bright. He runs and finds a stick, brings it back to her, and drops it at her feet.

"He's fine in every other way."

"Maybe he's just fasting."

"Dina, please . . . can we hold off on the horseback ride? It's wonderful you found it and everything."

"We already promised we're coming back next year, then we'll have a whole month. Maybe we can do three or four days or a week-long trip." Dina smiles.

AS THEY HIKE to Mt. Edith Cavell, their young legs scale the inclined trail faster than the families with kids, and some of the older people who look hopefully ahead for benches to rest on. One of these seems familiar and Tessa does a double take as the tall older woman crosses the path just in front of them.

"Madeline?"

"Oh my word. Tessa. How miraculous." Madeline hugs Tessa. "So nice to run into road friends."

"This is Dina."

"Well hi, Dina. What brings you up the mountain today?"

"We heard there were flowers in bloom up on the shale part."

"Ah, lucky you. I'm afraid to walk on the shale anymore. But isn't this sight just amazing?"

They all look up as a distant thundering indicates a small avalanche of snow cascading gracefully into Mt. Cavell's emerald green glacial pool.

"This is one of my most favorite sights in the world. If you ever get a chance to read about Edith Cavell be sure to do it. Fascinating history. Remarkable woman."

"Are you staying at the Provincial Park?" Tessa asks, as Dina wanders to the next curve.

"Indeed I am. Look me up, will you? Oh. We don't know what each other's rigs look like, do we? Hmmm. Oh, I don't want to hold you two up, your friend seems restless."

"No worries." Tessa writes down her phone number.

"We'll be here a few days, then I take Dina to Edmonton for her flight out."

"Okay, let's be sure to look each other up. Enjoy the view."

"It's great seeing you, Madeline." Tessa embraces her. She hesitates, then passes on what she wants to say: All the sights she's seen and the people she's met. "Soon."

MT. EDITH CAVELL in all her glory faces Madeline. Madeline watches the two young women frolic from shale, to sub alpine and marmots and mountain flowers, to the green pool of the glacial waters and mini avalanches. They've done it in a third of the time it would take her.

Envying their young flexible knees and hips, Madeline figures in a tenth of the time it would take her. How easy they seem to scale the shale, no worries about being too far away from a bathroom.

Madeline sighs and listens to the quiet roar of mini avalanches falling down the face of Edith Cavell as she remembers an earlier time, and a younger body, and making love in the sun. She laughs, even as a tear falls on her cheek.

"HONEY? IS IT okay if I take the truck and run into Jasper? I need to send this last assignment to Dr. Lynch."

Everything is almost back to normal with Dina. Almost. Dina has brought up the horseback ride two more times, maybe they could go for just an afternoon? Tessa agrees this might be a good compromise, but peevishly she's still angry about the loss of Sadie in the last campground. And the fact she still has yet to return for the ash drop at the Saskatchewan River.

"Sure."

"I'll be gone two hours, tops. By the way, the light over the bed went out again."

"It has to be a loose wire. Maybe it's that mouse I saw crawling around . . ."

"Mouse? Ewwww."

Tessa investigates the light, first changing the bulb to make sure it isn't blown. She checks the circuit by flipping the other light that's on the same line with it. Paul had done a quick run through the first time she met him on how to trace the lights. He said rodents seemed to like these best.

She pops the trim over the wiring and examines the insulation on the wire, then she pops the second piece of trim. A baggie and an old-fashioned silver teaspoon handle fall out. The teaspoon has a roach clip soldered on the end where the spoon part should be. Tessa unrolls the skinny baggie. A pot stash!

"Auntie! I crossed the border with this!" Tessa's heart is beating really fast. She decides to put this away, unsure if she'll tell Dina about it, just yet.

Tessa returns to the wire. Where the silver tool and baggie have been riding, a small fray on the insulation exposes copper wire, just enough to make contact intermittently.

"Auntie, auntie, auntie," Tessa says, as she takes black electrical tape and wraps the broken insulation. Would this old soul ever quit surprising her? What other secrets did the rig hold?

CHAPTER 23

TESSA WATCHES DINA pour a second drink. Dina is oblivious. She is consumed with the idea that she is being replaced while on vacation. That the lead professor has found someone else more reliable. She is fretting she is losing status at college.

"Why did I take so much time?"

"Do you need to return?"

Dina looks at her with new hope. "I knew you'd understand."

"But I don't understand. It's only five more days."

"But this is my life. This is my whole life. People are counting on me and I'm not there."

"It doesn't make sense to change everything for just a few days."

"This is cutthroat academic level. If I'm not there when the need arises . . . poof . . . I'm out. Just like that. Do you really want me just inputting data on some archaic program for my Masters and Ph.D.? I'll be relegated to the outside. I won't be on the cutting edge. There's so much pressure. But you don't get it."

"Why do you do it, if there's so much pressure?"

"Because, I love the competition. I love being on top." Dina's eyes are blazing.

Tessa is unsure if it's Dina talking or the alcohol. No matter what Tessa says, it's not right.

"Oh, sweet pea. It's not that I don't love you. Of course I do. I'm sorry. It's just that I can't help thinking if I had a better Internet connection, I could know for sure if Dr. Lynch is trying to reach me."

"Maybe we should drive down to Jasper."

"Can we?"

"Sure."

"And then we can have dinner there, okay? I'll buy. My treat."

Tessa opens the door of the truck, letting Murphy jump into his day bed.

"Does Murphy have to come?" Dina asks. "It's an awful long ride for the dog."

"That's just it. If it's too long, he might need to go out and we're a couple of hours away."

"Well, you have a point."

On the way down, Dina is effusive with her love and affection. "Once I know Dr. Lynch doesn't really need me, then I can focus on just us." She's returned to being jovial Dina, full of laughter and energized.

TESSA DRIVES TO Jasper because it makes Dina happy and Dina talks about everything else but school. She talks about when they will be living together and they'll have gardens and rocking chairs on the front porch. They laugh about growing old together, and maybe one day having kids.

At dinner, as they wait for a call back from Dina's professor, Dina leans across the table, her eyes smoky and full of love. "You know, it's too bad you didn't keep what you were born with. We could have had the whole package."

Stunned, Tessa says nothing. Sure, Dina had two drinks before the ride down here. And yes she's had two glasses of wine, but she's not slurring her words, nor does she seem drunk. But she has just said the absolute worst thing she could have ever possibly said to Tessa.

A little bit of Tessa dies.

Dina puts her hand over Tessa's, right there in public.

Dina, the one so afraid of being out. She seems to suddenly realize what she's said. "I mean we *could* have kept . . ."

"No," Tessa says flatly and pulls her hands away.

She shakes her head. No.

No!

She can't talk. She can't make a sound. A gurgle comes out but says nothing. She pushes her chair back and rushes out of the restaurant and blindly walks down the street, looking for the truck. Tears flood her eyes so quickly, she looks the way she hears traffic is coming and sees round, ocular, lights through the distorted lens of her tears, headlights far away, and runs for the cement median in the center of the four lanes, runs for the parking lot she thinks the truck is in, runs from everything Dina has just broken . . .

"Tessa!" She hears Dina in the far off distance and steps off the median curb, very nearly being hit by a car. Horns honk and people stop and Tessa runs runs runs, crying, sobbing, fleeing.

NOOOOOOOOOOOOOOOOOOOOOOO

NOOOOOOOOOOOOOOOOOOOOOOOO

NOOOOOOOOOOOOOOOOOOOOOOOO screaming inside her.

She fumbles with the keys at the truck and it's just enough time for Dina to catch her.

Murphy is nosing the driver's window, his tail up, alert . . .

Dina grabs her from behind, her arms locked around her.

"No." Tessa is sobbing and falling against the door. "No." She is falling to her knees, crying sobbing melting unmoving, her gut shot through.

No

No

No

Dina is on the wet pavement with her. "Baby, baby, baby. I'm sorry. I'm sorry. I didn't mean it like that. Baby, please."

Tessa howls like her soul has been ripped out.

Her heart breaking into a million pieces of glass, shredding anything left whole in her chest.

THEY ARE TRAVELING back to the rig in silence. Dina is driving.

Tessa is numb, Murphy's head lies in her lap and she is petting him without stopping. Petting him so she's grounded.

To her credit Dina says nothing more. That night.

In the morning, Dina slides wordlessly from her self-imposed exile on the couch into Tessa's arms. Tessa holds her as the small of Dina's back pushes gently into her tummy. They spoon.

In her head Tessa is hearing, "It'soverit'soverit'sover." But she keeps her heart steady by counting one, two, three, four

Over

And over

And over.

When the sun has risen high enough, and it's time to let Murphy out, Tessa shifts and Dina moves to a seated position. Tessa is acutely aware of Dina's eyes on her back as she slides on her cold damp Levi's.

Tessa does not look up when she says, "I'll be back." And closes the door.

She walks Murphy to the back part, beyond where the elk were sleeping the afternoon before and stops short of the pine trees where bears have scratched the pine bark off with long swipe marks, exposing naked yellow flesh of pine and bubbled sap. The deep grooves of sharpened bear claws shredding the fat of the pine tree, belly split wide open.

She returns to the campsite, and Dina is at the picnic table, smoking a cigarette.

Dina doesn't smoke cigarettes.

Her eyes are red rimmed and she looks the way Tessa's insides feel.

Tessa sits at the picnic table as Murphy laps water from his bowl. He comes and rests under the picnic table with a soft "Hummpph."

It's the most anyone's said all morning.

"I can't take it back." Pragmatic. That's Dina.

"And I can't change who I am."

But you have.

The unspoken.

"I'm finally who I've always been and my body matches me."

"I know." Dina nods. "It was a stupid, selfish thing to say."

It was much more than that.

But Tessa remains silent. She's afraid whatever little bit is holding her together will dissolve if she tries to understand any more than she can bear right now.

In some form, without words, the rest of their morning is spent readying Dina, and her laptop and the career she so desperately wants, to leave.

TESSA RETURNS FROM the hotel in Jasper. From there an airport shuttle will deliver Dina to Edmonton for her flight home. As soon as Tessa enters the rig, Murphy begins eating. She looks at him with hollow eyes and attempts some humor. "Well, at least one of us can eat."

CHAPTER 24

MADELINE WALKS BY the camper that night, hoping to catch the girls outside. Instead she hears muffled sobs. She hesitates knocking, but she hears a small sigh escape, like the last little bit of air, from a balloon.

"Just a minute."

Tessa's eyes are bloodshot and her hair is pushed in all different directions from having her face buried in her pillow. She has very dark circles around her eyes.

"Maddy. I look awful. I know."

"May I come in?"

"Yes." Tessa snuffles.

Murphy lies by the bed and looks at Madeline. Madeline sits at the table, struck by Murphy's almost human eyes. They look like they are saying, "Help! Please."

It's obvious to Madeline that what was once two is now one.

Tessa looks raw. She suddenly jumps up. "I need to offer you tea."

"Sit, please. I take it this has something to do with that young woman I met earlier this week?"

Tessa nods.

Madeline resists saying anything right away. She gives Tessa time to absorb her presence.

"I had my heart broken like that once," she said softly.

"Y-you?" Tessa glances at Madeline's silver engagement and wedding rings.

Madeline thumbs the rings. "Oh, yes. I've loved and lost. You can't live this long and not."

"How do you get through it? I thought this was it. I thought . . ." Tessa looks at the ring on her second finger and twists it, but not removing it yet.

Madeline recognizes her struggling with not wanting to admit it's all over. "Everyone selects their own path. But I can tell you it gets better."

"With time." Tessa says it by rote.

"No. It gets better, because there is someone better for you. Someone who will respect you and lift you. Someone who will accept you just as you are and not want to change you."

"Promise?"

"Yes. I know you didn't ask for my advice, but I'm giving it. Go through this grief. Feel it. Don't numb it or push it down or," Madeline hesitates, "be with the last person who made a pass at you and settle for them. That won't work. It never does. It's predicated on bad ground. Trust me. One day it won't be so intense. It won't be every hour. And one week, it won't be every day."

Tessa looks like she's absorbing this. "I'm thinking about the surgeries I went through," she whispers. "Sometimes the pain was so intense, but the less painkillers I took, the faster I healed."

Madeline nods. "The healing is in the mountains and water around you now."

"And some people." Tessa looks at Madeline.

"Why thank you."

"And Murphy." Murphy sits up and goes to Tessa.

"And Murphy," Madeline agrees.

THE NIGHT DINA left, and the next night, Tessa cries herself to sleep. When she finally sleeps she has disturbing dreams.

Most of them are about wet, slimy ground, or surfaces

she can't run on, Jell-O-like ground, unstable. Being in an earthquake. She tries to run and things grab her. A stick leaps out of nowhere and she trips and falls, thorny bushes tug her clothes and scratch her legs. Holes open on what used to be reliable ground. Nothing is certain or stable.

Sometimes she can't move and she's caught, like a rabbit in a snare, like a coyote in one of her father's traps.

Her head snaps up.

The coyote traps and a memory spills out of the wide open crack in her head and her heart.

Trudging through the snow that day, the wet, sloppy, yucky snow with her dad and Eli.

Her dad saying, "C'mon, T, pick up your feet. You act like you're in a tar pit. You too, Eli."

"I don't want to be doing this," Tessa says.

"Tough shit. It's time you become the man you're meant to be, Teddy."

Tessa throws down the coyote traps. "I'm not Teddy! I never was."

"Dad, let it go," Eli says.

"Shut up, Eli. Stay out of it." Their father swings and the slap to Eli's face explodes and echoes up the long valley they are climbing.

Horrified, Tessa sits up.

She's remembering. She can't remember. Not now.

She shoves it away. Instead, she starts thinking, "When was the last time I ran?"

She throws on her shorts and shirt and laces up her shoes. She leashes Murphy to her waist, she begins to run. It must be after midnight, because it's the darkest she's ever seen it. Even so, a perimeter of light rims around the portion of sky between the mountains and the trees. As she runs she wonders, "Does it ever really get dark here?"

And when she sees the entire circumference of the rim of light she knows it's a light that won't stop coming in until she remembers everything in every minute detail.

And then it happens.

About as far away from the rig as she can be.

She twists her ankle.

"TESSA?" MADELINE APPROACHES her.

Tessa looks up from wrapping her ankle and ducks her head.

"What happened?"

"I went for a run last night."

"Couldn't sleep?"

Tessa shakes her head, fighting back tears. "And then this fucking happens. About as far away as I could get."

"Oh no. You must have felt so all alone."

"It took me a long time to return. I found a stick and used it, but . . ."

"Honey, you should have called me."

"I didn't have my phone with me. Anyway, it's not your responsibility . . ."

"I know, but we all need someone, sometimes. What about calling your mother?"

"You mean for her to come here?"

Madeline nods.

"She can't afford to take time off work."

Because of me. Because of selfish me. Uncle Chuck the fuck is right.

Madeline doesn't argue. She just sits with her.

"I have to drive back to the Saskatchewan River."

"Do you want company?"

Tessa considers this a moment.

"No." After the argument with Dina she only scraped

together enough ashes for two, maybe three, more ash drops, tops. "Thank you. I'd just as soon go alone."

AFTER MADELINE LEAVES, Tessa looks at herself in the mirror. Suddenly, without thinking, she opens the drawer. She removes a pair of scissors. She looks at her image again. Taking a thick lock of her hair in her left hand, she caresses it. She suddenly clenches it. She takes the scissors and cuts, just below her ear lobe.

She lets the dark, chestnut tress fall, as she methodically cuts, all the way around. Some length of the pink and blond hair join the mass that looks like a small animal at her feet.

She finishes, gathers all the hair up, and ties a band at each end. She holds the length of hair in each hand, her palms a good six inches apart. She is surprised by the weight of it. The heft of this.

It is the first time she's had short hair since . . .

She shoves that memory away.

For a moment she holds what was just her.

That Tessa is gone.

TESSA DRESSES SLOWLY like she is drenched in molasses for the last of the big three hikes in Canada to disperse the ashes. Lethargic, slow, methodical. She opts leaving the iPhone in the rig. She texts Mr. Forsythe and tells him what she's doing, that she missed the ash drop. That she only has enough ashes for the next two drops. She doesn't explain how it happened.

Just this once, she wants to be unfettered and free. Untangled. Unreachable. She breaks down in tears, collapsing to a sitting position on the floor, her ankle throbbing. Murphy is licking her tears. Special abilities.

Who is she crying for? The family that would be disappointed she missed all those east stops because of Chuck? Herself because of Dina? She almost calls her mom, but her mom is focused on making sure Eli's freedom is secured. She doesn't want to burden her about Dina, about the fight, about anything.

Murphy, at least, can still go with her. She rereads Forsythe's river explanation. "The Columbia River takes the ashes to the Pacific Ocean, the Saskatchewan to the Atlantic, the Athabasca River to the Arctic Ocean. This one section of drops alone is your Aunt Sadie's greatest wish fulfilled."

Good, because there isn't much left for any other drops.

She'd check in with Mr. Forsythe later. She's blown her college tuition. The family will be pissed. Something will be worked out. Her mom, Eli, and she will undoubtedly be cut out of everything. She's failed Eli and her mom. Again.

"So easy a task and you managed to fuck that up too."

She hears Chuck's voice in her head.

She won't be able to defend herself. She can't tell the truth about the ashes to the rest of the family, maybe to her mom one day. But not now. Her mom never trusted Dina to begin with. She's unsure what she can do anymore. Now she can only hobble with the cane that Madeline had provided her.

She remembers the athletic man she met on Stone Mountain, and she takes a moment to find the lime green bike cap he gave her. She pulls her pink forelock out, still long enough to show under the backside brim that she wears in front. She moves forward. Determined.

CHAPTER 25

TESSA RETURNS FROM the river and puts her ankle up and ices it with one of the two bags she bought at Saskatchewan Corners. She distracts herself from the pain, with the photo albums. She finds the picture of the four of them in 1968 at Lake Louise, Lake Agnes Tea House. The four of them. She looks again. That can't be . . . That can't be.

Tessa finds Madeline at her camper.

Madeline smiles. "Honey? Did you cut your hair?"

Tessa touches her shortened locks. Nods.

"Mmmm. I used to be a hairdresser in a former life. Sit."

Tessa obeys. She has a question she needs answered anyway.

Madeline returns from the rig with a drape and a pair of shears. "Some folks actually pay me to do this on the road. This one is gratis. We'll just even up some of those layers you have going. My you cut it short. But you have beautiful, thick hair. I bet it grows fast."

The memory is flooding back: Her father taking the scissors and a fist full of her long, little girl hair . . . Tessa shoves it away again.

"Why, darling, you have some natural body here, this is going to be beautiful."

"You know," Tessa says carefully," I found pictures of my Great Aunt Sadie and Uncle Percy, when they were younger."

"Did you?"

"Mmhmmm. And there's another couple with them. Right here. In Canada."

"Is there?"

"That's you, isn't it?"

"Well, I'd have to see the picture."

Without hesitation Tessa pulls out the color photo she has in her pocket. It's the two couples at the Tea House above Lake Louise.

Madeline glances at it. "Yes, that's me."

"You didn't even look at it. You've been following me this whole time, right?"

"Well, no, not exactly."

"Mr. Forsythe send you? He paid you to follow me, right?"

"No one paid me to do anything."

"Then why? Why are people following me? Why doesn't anyone think I can do this myself?"

"It's not that, honey." Madeline smiles, her arm bent at the elbow, the scissors up in the air as she bends forward and looks Tessa in the eyes. "It's that your Uncle Chunk is such a dick."

Tessa laughs, despite her focus on all this new information. "But who are you? And who is this other guy in the picture?"

"I will be happy to answer every single one of your questions, but frankly I'm famished. After I finish evening up some of these edges, why don't you return to your rig and make one of those fabulous salads you rave about and I will tell you everything. Promise."

And for a moment, Tessa realizes she hasn't been feeling the drowning, or drama of emotions involving Dina. For a brief moment, she's allowed herself the respite of being authentic in the moment. It's going to take practice. She needs to do this to heal.

"Okay."

"I need protein, none of that vegan stuff for me. And bring that fine ax you have in the camper, I need to split some wood for our campfire tonight."

Madeline makes a few more snips. She mousses Tessa's hair with some product and professionally hands her a mirror.

"Wow. You left most of the pink."

"I like the pink. Are you happy?"

"You make me look hot."

"That's not hard to do, sweetie. So, you like?"

"Very much."

"Good, now don't dawdle making the salad, okay?"

Tessa obeys and makes her spinach, feta, tomato, hard-boiled egg, avocado, and walnut salad.

Madeline insists on grilling.

Tessa is also dragging the ax behind her. She can't put her finger on it, but she hates axes. This one looks like it's been in the family for generations. It has an old sturdy wood handle with the patina of human oils and rubbed-in varnish. Inscribed in neatly carved, cursive, charcoal black letters is "Babe."

Tessa believes it must be the name of the ax, or Uncle Percy's nickname, like on the back of the photograph.

Madeline picks up the ax and begins splitting wood. She catches Tessa watching her, almost open mouthed.

Madeline grins, her beautiful dimples creasing the corner of her mouth and without saying a word stacks a chunk on another big round piece of wood and lifts the ax in the air. It slices smoothly through the wood like butter.

"The trick is eyeballing that splinter piece you want and not biting off more than you can chew."

Thwack.

Another straight piece falls off like a fat pat of butter.

"It helps that it's ash wood also." Now Madeline is downplaying her prowess. "And I've done it since I was a kid." She thumbs the edge of the ax. "Huh."

That one movement triggers a freight train of barreling memories for Tessa. While Madeline is absorbed with taking a rasp from her tools, filing the burr off the axe head, Tessa is plunging into a series of picture memories she can't stop.

Thwack.

Blood.

She buries her hands in her face.

"Ohmygod. Ohmygod. Ohmygod." She is keening and rocking back and forth. Her face in her hands.

Alarmed, Madeline abandons her task and turns Tessa from her seat at the picnic table toward the mountain. Murphy is sniffing at Tessa, whining.

"Ohgodohgodohgod." Tessa is holding her stomach. Holding her stomach so her guts won't fall out. Holding her stomach where the deeply hidden searing resides, and is now roaring to her forehead, unleashed. "I killed him! I killed him!"

Madeline pulls her in and Tessa leans against her, against the taller, stronger body, against her chest. She collapses within the surprisingly strong arms and dissolves.

Her head is pounding and she's gagging. Madeline insists she drink water. She pours water on a dishcloth and puts it on Tessa's neck, one arm still holding her.

After the nausea passes, Madeline helps Tessa into her camper. She leads Tessa back to the bed and puts the cool cloth over her forehead.

"Ever since Dina left, I've been having nightmares. Now I understand them."

"Don't jump to conclusions. Traumatic events can shift your sense of what really happened."

"My dad backhanded Eli and then he punched me."

Tessa closes her eyes as it all comes rushing back.

It had been just that quick, her dad backhanding Eli and turning with a closed fist to punch her, once, twice. She partially covered her face and before he could hit her again, she could see Eli jump on her father's back and begin pounding him, howling.

Their father threw him off. "Is that all you got?"

He spat a stream of tobacco juice that landed near Eli's head in the snow.

Eli roared and ran at him again. Their father was still holding the knife but it was behind his forearm as he shoved Eli off with both hands. Eli went face first in the dirt and snow.

"You were always the slow one."

Eli got up on all fours and was looking at Tessa, but not really. Her head was exploding from her father's fist but she could see Eli's eyes. They were fixed somewhere else and almost seemed to be turning into yellow cat eye slits. Cold, pure hate, not at her, but at him.

Their father toed Eli's behind with a boot. "Try again."

Eli howled and turned. He grabbed their father around the knees. He pulled them into the wet leaves and snow. They tussled and turned and fought. Wrestling, sticks broke under their heaving bodies. Their father was on top, his forearm against Eli's throat, the knife still gripped in his right hand, tucked away from Eli's face.

He was choking Eli with a rage that was out of control. "I brought you in and I can take you out!"

Eli's feet were kicking and he was losing; Tessa heard horrible rasping, choking sounds. She was up, the ax in her hands, and it was just that quick. She closed her eyes and swung, connecting.

The side of her father's face fell away as he rammed his right arm back at whatever had attacked him and cut under the hem of Tessa's green, wool jacket. Her eyes fly open and their father's momentum took him all the way around, the disfigured monster.

Tessa fell.

Madeline is looking at her with large, brown eyes, absorbing this story.

Tessa begins sobbing. Big, racking grief-stricken cries.

She remembers. She remembers all of it and hates herself. "I killed my father, Madeline. I did it. Uncle Chuck is right. I'm no good. I'm a bad seed. I murdered my father."

"You know, honey. Memory can be a funny thing. This trauma with your girlfriend . . ."

"Ex-girlfriend." Tessa sobs.

"Yes. Ex-girlfriend . . ."

"I did it. Not Eli. All these years I was thinking it was him. And he took the fall for me. He took the fall for me because he knew what it would cost . . ." Tessa tears soak Madeline's lap.

Madeline strokes her hair.

"I didn't think this could get any worse."

"Don't you think the trauma with your gir . . . ex-girlfriend provoked this?"

"Maybe."

Madeline lets Tessa cry as long as she needs.

"Is there any possibility this might be what you think happened, instead of what really happened?" Madeline asks.

Tessa searches inside her brain. She sees it all clearly. She shakes her head no. "What now?"

"Well, I think a drink would be nice, don't you?"

"I mean, do we go to the cops?"

Tessa hears Madeline chuckle.

"Why?"

"Well, 'cause . . ."

"Oh no, child. Whatever for? Land sakes, has civilization eroded this far we have to depend on authorities more than our souls?"

"But if I . . ."

"Tessa," Madeline takes both of Tessa's hands in hers,

"hear me now. Whatever happened, whatever you did or think you've done . . . What was your intent?"

"To save Eli."

"And did you?"

"Yes."

"Then all else fall's to the side. You need to wait some. And get home and return to familiar. You've been on the road almost three months, doing other's work. And this fight with your girlfriend . . ."

"Ex-girlfriend."

"Ex-girlfriend hurt you. The first is always the hardest."

Tessa's eyes widen. "You mean this happens more than once? I can't go through this twice."

"Then I suppose three or four times would be out of the question?"

Tessa pulls her hands away and folds her arms over her face. "Oh god, this sucks."

"I agree, it does. Don't hide your grief any more than you would your love."

"I'm not."

"And when you're done, I'll tell you all the stories you want to hear."

Madeline hands Tessa a wad of Kleenex. Tessa blows her nose so loudly it sounds like a goose honking as it takes flight and startles Murphy.

"Do you need a neti pot?"

"A what?"

"To irrigate your nose."

"No. I don't think so."

"Honey. Just take a moment and breathe, can you do that for me? Big, deep breaths."

Tessa straightens and closes her eyes, listening to Madeline's breathing slow and sure, coaching her.

Madeline does three long breaths.

Tessa adds a fourth. Murphy leans against her. Tessa opens her eyes and turns to him. She holds his long face in her hands. “You are my rock, aren’t you?” She looks at Madeline. “I’m sorry to burden you with all of this.”

“It’s what friends do. I care about you, Tessa Marie.”

Tessa pauses. “How did you know my middle name is Marie?”

“Maybe I heard your friend say it.”

“I don’t think so.”

“Oh, well then . . . busted.”

“Busted?”

“That’s going to have to wait. I think you’ve been through quite enough for one day.”

“Then tell me about you and the man, in the picture.”

“That man in the picture is my husband.”

“Where is he?” Tessa puts a hand over her mouth. “He’s not dead, right?”

“No!” Madeline laughs. “My husband’s name is Dan.” A smile tugs at the corner of her mouth. “His full name is Dan Forsythe.”

Tessa feels her mouth drop open. “But you said your last name is Sweet.”

“It is. My maiden name. Dan and I are . . . separated.”

“Yeah. He’s in Michigan and you’re here.”

“No. I mean we haven’t lived together for a very long time.”

“Oh.”

“Like years.”

“So you sorta babysat me ’cause you’re on the road all the time?”

“No, I’m more like a human guardian angel. You didn’t see Chuck after that night in Ottine, did you?”

“That was your doing?”

“I had some help.”

“The Hoopers? You all acted like you didn’t know each other on the ferry . . .”

“Yes, we did. I’m glad we were so convincing. Chris is a former Navy Seal. He is very commanding when he need be.”

“Chris? He was all freaked out about the shotgun.”

“Chris is a good little actor, isn’t he?”

“And now you’re here . . . ?”

“Well, because of Dina.”

“So why are you here because of Dina?”

“Call it a hunch.”

“A hunch?”

“A sixth sense.”

“A sixth sense like she was going to say something totally shitty and break my heart? That kind of sixth sense?”

“Yes.”

“Are you a mom?”

“No. I am so not a mom.”

“I’m exhausted.”

“Well, you’re not going anywhere till we have supper, okay?”

Tessa nods.

“Now do me a favor, please, and rest a bit. Drink more water. Come outside when you’re ready.”

Madeline has a look on her face that Tessa doesn’t argue with.

Tessa lies back down in the big, comfortable, queen size bed of the motorhome.

She tries closing her eyes, but that seems to last only a moment. She opens her eyes, and is surprised that time has actually passed. Not only is Murphy’s warm body beside her, the sun light in the window has shifted over, illuminating a framed piece of embroidery on the wall near the foot of the bed that says, "Into your garden you can walk and with each plant and flower talk."

Curious, Tessa rises and investigates the walls of the rig.

There's a cloth patch with a black border and red background pinned on the wall by the bathroom door. A campfire in the middle with the words in black stitching above and below, "We are the Grand Daughters . . . Of all the witches you were never able to burn."

Wow.

Tessa walks toward the front part of the coach.

A bumper sticker is stuck to the fabric behind the driver's seat and over the couch. It has a piano in the trees and says, "See you in August."

Over the driver's seat is a large pink banner with #moranstrong and a photograph of a woman racer crossing the finish line in a lime green shirt, arm's upraised in elation. She exudes joy.

Madeline calls in. "Tessa? Are you awake?"

"Yes."

"The grill is hot. Will you please pull the meat off the center shelf in the fridge?"

Tessa opens the door and pulls out a very neatly wrapped packet in white butcher paper with black handwriting reads, "Chuck steak."

Tessa stares at the packet and slowly walks out of the camper to Madeline.

"Honey, you look like you've seen a ghost."

Tessa hands her the packet, her eyes never leaving the hand written "Chuck."

Madeline bursts out laughing. "I did not pull a *Fried Green Tomatoes*. Promise. That really is chuck steak."

THE NIGHTS WITHOUT Dina are incredibly lonely. Tessa has no one with which she can make a goodnight tuck-in call. Or process the whole scene with her father, her, and Eli. Eli. Eli will tell her. Eli will tell her everything. Madeline is right. She needs to return home.

For now, it's just her and Murphy. At one point she goes out to look at the stars that fill the sky. It must be after one and before four, because the sky is black. Far off she hears a sound like tinkling water and she wishes the Northern Lights would come.

IN THE MORNING, Tessa runs.

Not very far because it feels like her bone is on top of her foot. But she forces herself to try. She knows she must look ridiculous to the other campers, with their families and friends, out in the morning sun, drinking coffee. Sharing laughs. And her trying to run, a hippity hoppy kind of run. She wears the lime green hat because it gives her strength.

She can't afford to care what others think. She stares at the beauty around her and forces herself to run. To hobble, to half ass jog. *Good. Let it hurt, let this pain be greater than the one inside.*

She maybe only gets a quarter mile, and then she turns around and hobbles back. She hears from behind her a tinkling noise, like rain against a metal roof. It's Madeline, wearing one of Great Aunt Sadie's ankle bracelets, made from antique buttons.

"You have one of Great Aunt Sadie's ankle bracelets."

"I do." Madeline sits at the picnic table and pats the seat next to her. "I haven't been completely honest with you. You didn't read far enough in those journals, did you?"

Tessa feels her cheeks warm out of embarrassment. The

days with Dina blew everything else in her world out of the water. She's looked at the pictures again, but not the journals.

"Your aunt and I had more than a friendship."

Tessa absorbs this. "You're B. In the journals."

"Yes."

"B, as in Babe."

"Yes."

"So that ax is yours?"

"We travelled together. It belongs with the rig."

"What about Uncle Percy?"

"Well, Dan and he had more than a friendship."

B and F. Forsythe. Fortie.

Tessa starts to say something. Madeline waits.

Tessa's mind is spinning. Madeline says nothing.

"I don't understand. Why stay married? Why did any of you stay married?"

"Don't judge us too harshly, honey. Things were really different even a few years ago. In the sixties and seventies, there were groups of women who would have parties, like for birthdays and they wouldn't even admit *among themselves* that they were couples. At least the groups that Sadie and I, and Dan and Percy would socialize with, we all admitted our couple-ness. It was like, when we all got together, we suddenly had more air to breathe. Sadie thought about burning all that stuff. The photos and the journals."

"I'm glad she didn't."

"Dan and Percy strongly recommended she should."

"I'm really glad she didn't."

"Dan and Percy told her it would only hurt other's feelings if they read them."

They sit quietly for a few moments.

"Things haven't changed for generations, then, it seems like a ski ride. Imagine riding in a horse and buggy when suddenly, civilization decides to hop in a luge. I can't believe how fast it has changed. A Pope as loving, humble, and intelligent as the one now? I'm still catching my breath. The truth is, we all really loved each other and cared about each other. As Dan said, we had no crystal ball to know who would be left standing and economically, it just made sense, because no matter what, we wanted everyone to enjoy their end of life, lovingly."

"And in your own way, you paved the way for all of us."

"In our own way, I guess, we did."

"And you knew I was considered two spirit?"

"I always knew you as Tessa. No more, no less. Do you believe you are two?"

"No. I am not two. I am one. I have always felt the way I am now. My body didn't always match, but inside, always who I am now. No different. Maybe I got caught in the transporter room? The lower half belonging to someone else?"

"*Star Trek*? What do you know about *Star Trek*?"

"I'm a big fan of the classic *Star Trek*. Like the DVD episode Great Aunt Sadie has of *Deep Space Nine* "The Kiss." And even the old, old TV *Star Trek*."

"Mmm. Did you ever see the episode of Uhura and Kirk kissing? That was another first kiss, interracial on TV. That one made conservative heads explode back in the day." Madeline chuckles. "My, it's good we've come a long way. I'm lucky to see it."

"Now that gay marriage is legal, would you and Great Aunt Sadie . . . ?"

"We actually did. We flew to Hawaii three years ago."

"You're a bigamist."

"I prefer to think of it as a widow, who is still married."

"You said the first time is always the hardest. Is that true?"

"Only because of age. Each loss is different, but don't

be afraid to fall in love again. Please. Don't let what you had with Dina spoil what you can have with someone else. Having a broken heart means breaking it wide open."

Tessa tries to replace the stabbing pain she's experiencing in her bones with the more positive airy-fairy idea. She decides it will take her some time. "It hurts horribly."

"None of your surgeries were easy, either. Did that pain last?"

"No." She considers. "The only pain that stayed is the one I swallowed and didn't remember till yesterday."

"A good reason to accept grief as it comes."

Tessa nods.

"Even if all your relationships end, being afraid of the depth of love, to try and avoid the pain of loss, only handcuffs you to not fully realizing your life. After all you've been through, even before you fell in love with Dina, do you really want to limit yourself? You don't strike me as that type."

"I don't think I'm in control." Tessa releases one long exhale. "I'm not one to limit myself. Life tries to do that too much, already. But I'm afraid I won't make good choices."

"Hmmm." Madeline looks up at the sky as if she's pondering some great notion. "I can't promise that you will find everlasting love. But, if it makes sense to you, this is what I believe: There is a divine order, much wiser than any one of us. When I just relax about everything, the universe brings people into my life that I might not ordinarily meet, or want to get to know, but in much of it, I learn exactly what I need."

"What you're saying makes total sense. But I didn't hear anything about being in love."

"I've had many loves. And many losses. What is wise about love? Even though chances are we will lose our animals before they lose us, does it stop us from loving them?"

"No."

"No. So love and live, laugh and grieve and get up and do it all over again. What are our options? To be a dried up old prune existing a safe and sanitized life or to skid into home plate and say, 'Boy that was one hell of a ride'?"

"I like the skidding."

"So do I."

They sit in silence, sharing the intimacy of the mountains encircling them, the soft breeze, and air they inhale together.

"I love you, Aunt Maddie." Tessa suddenly hugs Madeline fiercely. She tucks her head under Madeline's jaw.

Madeline nestles into Tessa's embrace and whispers, "Oh, Tessa, I love you too. You're just perfect."

THAT NIGHT, TESSA rummages through her last mail drop. She had been in such a rush to pick up Dina, she barely took time to read everything. Now, she finds Prince's letter, and re-reads it more thoroughly.

> I hope this catches you in time. Thanks for giving me the General Delivery in Seattle. Tessa, my time with you on the Mississippi came at the perfect moment. I had no idea you had gone through the same change I had. It helped so much to speak with someone who totally gets it. I could have fallen in love with you!

After kayaking, Prince had helped Tessa locate a campground and she offered to cook dinner. He had agreed. They shared a closeness, but Tessa couldn't put her finger on it. It was vague, not attraction, more of a bond, like a brother.

At dinner, the flickering campfire played with the features

on Prince's face. He was crouched, his arms wrapped around his knees, watching the flames.

"My name used to be Jayda." He glanced up fearfully.

In the firelight Tessa could almost see the girl he once had been, but not really. It was like, in the briefest second, his face didn't have stubble on it. Like when the waves washed over rocks, at first the underwater landscape was so clear and then a shimmering took over and the features changed into some sort of impressionistic painting, a series of separate dots up close, but from a distance a cohesive whole. When all was calm, the features resumed their original place.

He was trusting her this far and he was holding his breath, as if waiting for a slap.

"And I used to be called Teddy."

They both grinned widely.

"Oh my god." Prince laughed. "We have transdar!"

He paused and shared another secret. "I'm attracted to guys."

"And I've pretty much decided I'm lesbian."

They smiled again.

"And people give you shit, right?"

"You're the first person I've told."

"Well, they will give you shit. They'll tell you, 'You were born the right sex to begin with.'"

"That has nothing to do with it."

"I know, right? But people can't wrap their heads around it. I wish, for just ten minutes, they would try being me, and all the shit I've gone through, to finally be comfortable in my own skin. Who would willingly put themselves through this much pain and crap? I hate taking drugs. Lots of First Nation people can relate, we call it Two Spirit. But it can mean more than us. It can mean women who are comfortable in their skin but want to do male things, or vice versa. It encompasses hermaphrodites. All sorts of differences."

"Well, that's interesting. What a cool way to deal with things as they are. I'm Sicilian, so traditionally, macho expectations." Prince shook his head. "I avoid those sort of stereotypes as much as possible. My male friends want me to be a macho dick; truthfully, when I first took the hormones? I was really quick to anger, but I don't like that behavior. I had a really excellent counselor guiding me through. Now I mentor newbies."

"That's really cool. What a great idea."

"I am so glad I met you. Can we stay in touch, as friends?"

"I'd like that," she said.

She returns to the letter in her hand.

> Do you think this happens in animals, only they can't change? When you said you learned that there's at least fourteen different variations from true male to true female, I was blown away. I think it's kind of ironic, that what is genetically considered true male and true female are sterile. Don't you find that odd? Don't you think the Universe really does want us to be somewhere in between, so we can be as strong as possible?

As strong as possible. Tessa isn't strong now, but the love in the letter from Prince heartens her and Aunt Maddie saying, sometimes you meet the people you are supposed to meet.

Tessa decides to FaceTime her mom.

CHAPTER 26

"AUNT MADDIE!"

Madeline turns from stowing the second arm of the awning and smiles. A warm glow starts up from her belly and fires into her heart every time Tessa calls her Aunt.

"Yes?"

Tessa stops in her tracks. "Are you leaving?"

"Oh, I never go very far. Just a little way down the road."

"But I wanted you and Mom to meet."

"I'm very glad you called her."

"You won't stay for a night and have campfire with us?"

"I thought, if it's okay with you, that once you are back in Michigan, I'll come then. Would that be all right?"

"Of course, I just thought it would be nice for all of us here."

"It's very special for you and your mom to have some one-on-one time. Another couple of weeks, I'll see you in Michigan." She pets Murphy as they sit one more time at the picnic table.

"Well, I wanted to ask you about this." Tessa proffers the teaspoon handle roach clip and small baggie.

"Oh my God. Where did you find that?"

Tessa tells her.

"That Sadie, I tell you, what an imp."

"Do you think it's any good?"

Madeline opens it. "Oh my, yes."

"Do you want it?"

"Oh good Lord, no. Neither Dan or I smoke. That was the hippy dippy Percy and Sadie routine."

Tessa laughs. "I don't really smoke either."

"Does your mother?"

"I don't know."

"Ask her. If she doesn't, you can always leave it somewhere for someone else, before you cross the border. Dan never would have allowed that if he'd known. Oh my God, he's going to shit when he finds out."

They both laugh.

"I love Dan, but he's too anal. Sadie was so opposite of him. My gosh, we certainly had some adventures. You keep that. And ask your mom and if not, someone on the road will appreciate the treasure you leave."

"I wanted to ask about something else."

Tessa relates the argument she had with Dina and the ashes being scattered.

"I don't have enough for the Bay of Fundy, or any of the eastern drops. I have enough for Idaho and Lake Superior."

"No worries." Madeline smiles. "I made those drops, myself, when you had to change course. You haven't failed the task, Tessa, if that's what you're worried about. You fulfilled it splendidly."

"I didn't want to fail Aunt Sadie, or Mr. Forsythe, even if that sounds weird."

"You succeeded beautifully, in every way. Take a deep breath and appreciate yourself for this achievement."

They each take a moment to look at the mountains encircling the site.

"Stay in my life? Please?" Tessa asks.

"I am delighted to be in your life, always."

IN HANA, WHEN it's time to bring the fish in, all the tribal villagers go down to the water to help. Elders sit up on the rocks above the water and direct the younger fishermen where the fish are.

It's a carnival atmosphere, smokes from food being cooked, some concessions sold, people look at each car to see who's arriving. An occasional tourist gets lost and finds themselves in the crowd. People aren't unkind, but they are not overly friendly either.

The nets come in and everyone helps sort. For their work, everyone is given part of the bounty and the rest goes to market.

Up on a hill, above Hana, is a large cross. Josh stands here, out of place, but not lost, overlooking the pastures, before he walks down to the water front. His long, youthful legs carry him effortlessly. He makes the transition from pasture to paved street as easily as he's made the transition from Northern Michigan to Hawaii. As easily as he did from Navajo country to Northern Michigan, as effortlessly as he breathes.

He strides down the tilting streets to the waterfront and walks into the fish coming in chaos. He understands tribal, community, stealing a car to harvest the parts for the good of the whole.

The dichotomy of the very rich and the very poor in Hawaii does not escape him. It's why he chooses to not live on an island, but he has a more immediate concern. He watches the men coming in. Their practiced legs stepping thigh deep in the cove's water, leading the boats in. Some men are big and round like Samoans, others are leaner, most are young, but some of the older ones who can still move well, heads down, nets in hand, lines from the vessels, walk the waters. One in particular.

Josh waits with the younger boys, and the women and children and some older men. The crowd is jovial and jostling and if they've noticed the taller younger man, they make no mention, except for a glance, and some of the teenage girls elbow each other as they sip from straws and plastic cups. Josh pretends not to see, but he smiles inside.

"Nadleh," he calls when the one he is looking for comes close.

The man's head snaps up, as if he's heard a sound from his past, from another life, a sound he's been waiting to hear again. His curly-topped black hair does not quite fit in here, and only once he's close do his features belie the dark tones of his skin. He could be native, or a dark European, a Mediterranean man. He hands off his nets and lines to someone on shore. And walks toward Josh.

"It's time."

The man nods and walks to another man his age in the water. The man in the water looks up at Josh and their eyes meet. They nod. The man in the water claps the other man's shoulder. The man closer to shore turns to leave with Josh, but not before a young boy comes up and hugs him around the thigh.

Gabe looks down and smiles. He tussles the boy's hair and, in a brief moment of affection, kisses him on the head.

As they leave Hana, Josh drives toward the barren side. Before they depart the green of the expensive cliffside homes, the public airport used for the ultra-rich people's private jets, Josh turns down a lane between two pasture fences and locates a small chapel.

He stops and goes inside. Gabe follows him. They let their palms run over the wood of the pews and inhale the air of many generations. For a moment, everything is still. For a moment, generations seep into their pores. They walk back out and behind to the cemetery. Josh walks to the edge of the cliff overlooking the water and watches the surf pound a rock out there. He watches the big curling waves loping in from an endless ocean, crashing and wending their foam and spit around this large plummeting rock. Then he moves back toward the grave he seeks and finds a large heart-shaped, dark grey it's almost black, rock right in the center of the other many large and black and grey island rocks rimming the square of this man's grave.

He bends down on one knee and removes the ash he carries in a small pouch. He lifts the rock and disperses the ash into the crevices below, marrying the soil of Hawaii with the soul of a woman he never knew with the ash of a doe he has slain. Rocks and crevices piled on so many others, and then he replaces the rock and reads the inscription.

> If I take the wings of the morning, and dwell in the uttermost parts of the Sea, even then Thine hand would lead me and Thy right hand envelope me.

"It's time," Josh says, standing and turning to Gabe. "It's time," he says again, with tears in his eyes.

CHAPTER 27

SHE WAITS FOR her mom at the Jasper Hotel, at the same place she'd dropped off Dina, not that long ago.

Tessa rushes to her and holds her fiercely. "It's so good to see you."

As her mother holds her, Tessa hears her whisper, "You've cut your hair."

"Yes."

Her mother runs hers fingers through the shortened thick hair. "It's almost curly." She looks at Tessa intently for a moment. "It's good being here."

They stand apart.

"And Murphy?"

"He's in the truck."

Her mom walks in a complete circle, looking at the sky and the mountains.

"What is it?"

"I don't think I've ever seen so much beauty in my whole life."

"Wait till you see Mt. Edith Cavell."

Tessa walks with her mom to the parking lot.

"You're limping!" her mom says as she looks at Tessa's taped ankle.

"It's getting better, really. Don't worry so much. C'mon." Tessa tugs her impatiently.

As they cross the street, Madeline's motorhome drives by and she honks.

Tessa waves.

"Who's that?" her mom asks.

"One of my new friends, Mom."

HER MOM IS driving, oohing and ahhing as she drives the rig south on 93a. Murphy's lying between them. Tessa looks at her mom.

"What is it?"

"Why did you divorce Dad?"

Her mom coughs. It's the kind of cough she does before she avoids a question. Not quite a lie and not quite the truth.

"We grew apart."

"No, Mom. Really."

Her mom's nervous tic comes out. The quick head shake. She lets out a sigh.

There you go.

"Honey, do you remember when you were young, I mean really young? When you told me about the seven sisters in the sky? When you said that your other people told you that the earth started out as a turtle?"

"Yes."

"You were about three then, and I wondered where did all these stories come from? You surprised us so much. Do you remember anything else?"

"I remember Eli and I thought we saw a face in the garage window pane, but I went to look and no one was there. We found a skeleton key when we tried to dig up Oreo."

Her mom nods. "Anything else?"

Tessa shakes her head.

"You told me, as soon as you could talk, 'You know I'm a girl inside, right?'"

"I don't remember that. I just remember always being a girl."

They ride in silence.

"Dad didn't like it."

"No."

"He more than didn't like it."

"That's why we traveled to your grandma and grandpa's. Not just to take them food."

"To bring them . . . me?"

"To receive their blessings and strength about you. Not only First Nation, but Athabascan. That's why we know Josh. Navajo comes from Athabascan, and he was sent to be near you."

"And we have both? Anishinaabe and Athabascan?"

"Yes. You, Eli, and me. We have both."

"What about Aunt Sadie and Uncle Percy?"

"Oh, honey, that's where it gets a bit different. Percy yes. Sadie, the rumor is, yes. She comes from the Crescent Side of North Manitou. She was adopted. And Percy is related to us by marriage."

They drive a little further. "Did you love Dad?"

"Yes. I loved him. I loved the Gabe I knew in college."

"What was he like, before you had us?"

"He was the most fun-loving man I had ever met. Always up for an adventure, smart, brilliant. Could build anything. He was the best father until . . ."

"I said I was a girl."

"It troubled him, at first. But he didn't focus on it. He thought it was a phase. He let it go until after his accident. Then, he became hateful about it, consumed by it. Perseverated about how we could cure you. He couldn't seem to distract himself. It was the accident that changed him. Not you."

"Mom," Tessa's voice catches, "I think I . . ."

"Don't say any more."

Her mom's jaw tightens as she continues driving. "I saw your blackened eyes, your stomach split wide open. He took closed fists to you, Tessa. He tried to kill you. You protected Eli, like you've always done. That's all that matters."

"Except Eli had to go to prison, while I was in the hospital. And you. I've cost you so much."

"You haven't cost me anything. This is life. This is what we do. We love each other and we go through things together."

"And Uncle Mark?"

"And Uncle Mark loves you as his own."

"Is he? Is he Eli's and my real Dad?"

"No, baby. He just wants to be, that's all."

IT'S IN HER dreams that her dad returns to her.

This time, mostly everything is all right. It's their weekend to be up north with him. Eli is sleeping in, but her dad rousts her and she eagerly goes with him. She's his pet.

Another adventure. They're in their farm clothes and the dad she loves says, "We are on a special mission. Only you and I can do this."

He seems so happy. It's fall time, the earth, their earth has started its tilt away from the sun. Orion is up early in the sky. The hunter. She can barely make out the edges of daylight.

"That sun will come fast. We have to hurry."

They get to the big farm where her dad sometimes works. They stop at the second silo.

"Slide over," her dad says. "You're going to follow me down."

She obeys him. She's driven his truck before, but not very often. Not for a mission.

He walks into the shed attached to the silo and the next thing she sees is him wheeling out a tractor with a big bucket on the front. A loader. He waves to her with a big smile and she follows. They return down the road they came from. They turn into a place where a small mobile home is parked.

He drives into a pasture with a pond behind it and shuts the tractor off. He motions for her to come. She shuts off the truck and slides out of the seat carefully. Her father's truck is big. It's hard for a ten year old to climb in and out. He comes to the door and holds it open. She doesn't see him pick something up from behind the seat.

They walk through the tall dying meadow grass.

"The sun is coming quickly," her dad says, again.

He opens a small dog gate and steps over an electric fence, about a foot off the ground.

"Careful," he says as she steps over the electric fence.

The shed they are at has a door jammed open by kicked up soft black dirt and to the right there's a spigot with gooey damp mud below it. It's a small pen.

"Where are you, Albert?" her dad calls. "Wake up. Breakfast. Stay back behind the door," he says to her as he goes in.

She hears a snorting and a rustling.

"C'mon, Albert," her Dad says in a friendly, conversational tone.

Then a big sleepy-eyed pig rambles out.

"Pet him on the head for a moment," her dad says, and she does.

He's a big pig, but friendly, and his little pig tail wags. Her dad gets some feed in a black well-worn rubber pan, and Albert happily follows him over to snuff and eat in it. Suddenly her dad moves her behind him, and he draws the small 410 to his cheek and takes aim at Albert's head.

Blam!

Albert falls and three-hundred pounds of pig trying to fight for his life levitates up and off the ground resoundingly three or four times. Like a whale breaching, slamming into the ground and the sound of him dying thumping up through the earth to her feet.

"Now the fun begins," Gabe says, and out of nowhere

he draws a sharp knife and steps expertly to Albert's head, avoiding the pig's thrashing hooves and body. He slices Albert's jugular. The blood sprays and hits the wire fence, droplets in the rising sun. A blood rain.

Horrified and sickened, Tessa presses her back against the door that doesn't move because of the jammed up earth. She isn't breathing. She squeezes her eyes shut and her hands sink into the soft black dirt. She hears birds calling from the pond as they lift off. Later, she will learn these are the calls of the sandhill cranes, about ready to migrate for fall.

Even though her eyes are closed, she can still hear Albert's breathing choking on his own blood as his massive fluttering body slows its huge drum thumping on the ground. The drum beats go down into the earth and the drum thumping comes up through her feet and into the space between her heart and her spine, all the way into her soul. Albert's waving whapping motion on the earth, like a fish out of water flapping at the landing, catches up to the last of his life leaving his body. Ceasing entirely in a matter of moments.

Tessa grapples at fistfuls of black dirt.

"What are you doing?" Gabe asks, mystified. "Where do you think the bacon we ate last night came from? C'mon now, T. Get up," he says, not unkindly, and pulls her to her feet.

"I have to have you run the loader so I can hook the chain to the bucket. Clean your hands off. Farmer White won't like dirt on the steering wheel."

Her mom holds her from this nightmare dream memory. She's trembling and shivering but can't feel the temperature. She can't feel anything. Her heart is frozen and she realizes she is still not breathing. One, two, three, four.

And why, at the end she sees Dina's face instead of her dad's is a mystery to her.

BETH WATCHES TESSA cry and is helpless. She strokes her head, as if petting Murphy. "It will pass, baby. I promise."

Beth puts a blanket over Tessa and tucks her in. Then she makes hot cocoa the old-fashioned way, with heavy cream, a touch of homemade maple syrup, and some cinnamon. Just enough maple syrup, so the organic ground cacao beans aren't bitter.

And after a time, Tessa sleeps. And when her daughter sleeps, all the wrinkled lines and puffy eyes relax, and Beth recognizes her baby girl once more, and is proud of the woman she's becoming.

THEY STOP FOR the night at the same campground where Dina saw the bear. They're still in British Columbia, making their way toward Idaho.

Tessa approaches her mom who is sitting at the picnic table on the edge of their campsite. They have a beautiful view of the mountain.

"Mom?"

"Yes?"

Tessa puts the joint in front of her mom.

"Oh, my!" Beth's eyes light up. Then she frowns. "Wait. Are you into drugs?"

Tessa cocks her head like Murphy does when he hears a strange sound. "Seriously, Mom? I like my lungs clear. I run. I found that."

Her mom looks at her doubtfully.

"Yep. In the garbage, back there." Tessa indicates one of the bear-proof bins. "Someone left it on a paper plate." It did happen, once.

"Well, how odd." Her mom picks it up and does a quick look around. They're secluded enough. "Maybe we should put it back?"

"Maybe we should smoke it."

"Tessa!"

"C'mon, you and Dad did it in college."

"Have you ever done it?"

Tessa rolls her eyes.

"Oh, that's right. I promised not to ask those kind of questions. This trip."

"We could just do a little bit and then I could put it back."

The campfire flickers. Beth picks up a thin stick and catches a flame on it.

"Well, I guess a little bit won't hurt."

"It's kind of a good sleep aid . . . right?"

"Sometimes." Beth inhales the first puff and passes Aunt Sadie's stash to Tessa. "Depends if this is Sativa or Indica."

Tessa inhales just a small amount and passes the joint back.

Beth takes a hefty inhale and then exhales. "In-dah-Coma."

They giggle.

"Ohhhhh. You know more than I thought."

Tessa inhales again and does a French curl, a technique where her exhale curls into her nose on a smooth inhale.

"Ooooooh, and I see you know a little more about inhaling then I thought." Beth starts coughing after her third hit. "Oh. That's enough for me." She hands it off to Tessa, who takes one more.

"That's enough for me too."

She stubs it out and looks at her mom questioningly. "Garbage?"

"Well. Let's wait and see if this works, okay?"

"Sure."

Tessa stashes it under a rock on the outside of the campfire.

"Oh. I haven't done that in a very long time. I've always loved the smell of it outdoors."

"Me too."

"You really don't do this a lot, right?"

"Mom . . ."

"I know. I'm being a mom."

"I hardly ever. But this is special. Our girls' trip."

"It is special."

Tessa decides to come clean. "I actually found this in the rig, when a light wasn't working. It's Aunt Sadie's."

"How do you know it's hers?"

"Because no one else would stash it there."

"It didn't taste old."

"Aunt Sadie took that trip to Dauphin Island last year."

"Oh yes. We were frantic, but she had a much younger friend with her . . . I can't remember her name . . ." Her mom starts giggling. She's almost hysterical, holding her chest. Then her eyes widen. "Oh, oh, oh . . ." She runs to the camper.

"Mom?" Tessa is right behind her.

"I just have to pee," her mom says before she dissolves in laughter again and makes it into the camper.

Tessa is grinning.

Beth's muffled voice comes through the bathroom door. "Oh, honey, I forgot how much fun that stuff is. Not that I'm condoning it."

"Of course not."

"I never would condone it."

"Strictly medicinal," Tessa says through the screen door.

"Yes. Medicinal."

They laugh.

"Did we pick up any ice cream last stop?" Beth is out of the bathroom, zipping up her shorts. She opens the freezer and squeals like a little child. "Chocolate!"

Murphy watches from under the picnic table. He licks his lips and sighs heavily.

Tessa looks back at him. She goes to the table, crouches down, and pets him. "Don't worry, you. We'll have play time tomorrow."

He picks up his head and wags his tail at the familiar words, *play time*. She reaches in her shorts pocket and finds a treat. "That's only fair, right?"

He gobbles it up. Ever since Dina left he's been back on his regular feeding schedule.

Tessa looks at him thoughtfully. "I need to listen to you better."

As the evening comes on, Beth drags out a sheet from the camper and Tessa lies with her as they look at the stars. Murphy lies next to Beth. His warmth is calming. Beth and Tessa entwine hands. "It's been so long, since I felt this young."

"You should always feel young, you're beautiful."

"I feel young now, and beautiful."

They both smile. A shooting star with a tail blaze of blue ignites the sky, searing an impression in the blackness.

"Wow!" they say in unison, then, "Aunt Sadie."

They look at each other and grin. Tessa rolls her head to her mother's shoulder. "You're always there for me."

"Always."

"Love you," Tessa murmurs, her eyes closing.

"Love you too." Beth rolls her head toward Tessa's, closing her eyes too. "Indica."

They both chuckle and snort, giggle and laugh on their blanket they call home.

And then, they share the quiet intimacy of a campfire, wrapped in unconditional love.

CHAPTER 28

IN IDAHO, THEY walk to the top of a lake by the eagle's nest and watch the eagle fish from the far shore.

Her mother stoops and exclaims, "Tessa, look!"

A magnificent long feather, black and white, flutters down onto the ground in front of them.

"She dropped one for us," her mom says, turning to her with bright eyes. She picks up the feather.

They shift from the ridgeline and continue to watch the eagle. She catches a fish in her talons and flies up to the nest and pecks at it, her head and beak working jackhammer like, till she gets a bit of food. Her head arches up as she swallows the food. She holds it momentarily before regurgitating it to her babies.

Tessa and Beth watch from a respectful distance away, the nest in clear view, little heads bobbing up to take the food from mom.

"Tessa? I have a question."

Tessa turns and searches her mom's face. "You can ask me anything. You know that."

"This one is hard. Before . . . you didn't want to talk about it." Her mom takes a deep breath. "The fact you are attracted to women." She is looking at the feather. Tessa watches her stroke the feather. "Is that part of who you were, before the surgery?"

Tessa smiles. Something inside of her has shifted, and she's unsure why, but now she can broach this topic and her mom, so fearful to ask, yet brave enough to ask anyway, deserves an answer.

"Mom, I've always been me." And then she uses the words Prince gave her. "My sexual identity is who I go to bed as. My sexual orientation is who I go to bed with."

Her mom looks into her eyes as the words sink in. "Then, I have one more. Do you love women because I hate men?"

This truth surprises Tessa as much as it seems to surprise her mom. Her mom puts a hand to her mouth, as if this truth just slipped out.

"Do you really hate men?" Tessa asks.

"I hate what some men do. What most men, do. They are cruel and unthinking." Her mom is looking down.

"Not all of 'em. Not Eli, not Josh. Not a lot of guys I've met."

"Well, maybe the younger generation is different."

"I love women, because . . . I love women. Truthfully? I've been with men. I'm just closer to women. It's not about the sex. It's about the connection."

"Even though she broke your heart?"

"A friend of mine says sometimes people break your heart . . . wide open."

"I just hate to see you in so much pain."

"I'm okay for a while and then I think about what we could have had. I think about this."

Tessa twists the ring off her finger and holds it out. It's the first time she's felt strong enough to remove it.

"It's a beautiful ring," Beth admits.

"And it was a beautiful promise. I thought she was my forever love." Tessa feels Aunt Sadie near. "I probably will cry more. I'm grieving. But, it's not every minute. It's not even every hour. With you here," she looks at her mom, "it hasn't even been every day."

The eagle skrees as she dives back toward the water for more food. They turn and watch her graceful, arcing flight as she hits the water and comes up empty, then flies up to a branch on a white pine tree near shore to watch diligently for her next catch.

"And pretty soon it won't be every week." She hugs her mom. "I'm so glad you're here."

"So am I, darling one."

THEY CONTINUE DRIVING Route 2 through Minnesota, Wisconsin, and the Upper Peninsula of Michigan. They arrive at the tip of the Keweenaw. They find a level site in the Fort campgrounds.

Tessa takes what is left of the ashes and divides them in two. She takes some of her cut hair to burn and float with the ashes.

"Let's take it in the vase this time," her mother suggests.

Tessa smiles. With her mother she needs to hide nothing.

They stroll along Lake Superior, right where Great Aunt Sadie and Percy had walked sixty years ago.

Her mother spies an agate. "Oh, have you ever seen one so pretty?" She touches it lovingly, fawns over it, and pockets it. She finds another rock, this one large and blood red from the iron ore in the water and removes an end of chalk from her pocket.

"Mom?"

"You don't mind I borrowed from your supply do you?"

Tessa shakes her head no and watches her mother curiously.

Her mom initials the rock with BW + TW. She places it, letters up, in the midst of other lettered rocks. People in every region have a different way of commemorating relationship. In Oregon, against the high sand walls of an undercut incline. In Arizona, the petroglyphs, in The Upper Peninsula on red rocks at the shores of Lake Superior. All along the way, Tessa recalls initials over a large boulder in New Mexico, carved in trees along the Mississippi near the Indian Marker trees. The Piasa and Thunderbird in the limestone cliffs. Whether present day or past, humans have made their scrawl, their mark—petroglyphs above pools of water outside Apache Junction, on train trestles and overpasses, on city walls, in caves in France.

"Now we are here forever." Her mom smiles.

Together they do the ceremony. Her mom uses the eagle feather they were given in Idaho, cleanses them both, and then indicates Tessa to take over.

"You're the Elder."

"You were given the ashes."

So Tessa acknowledges the four directions. She gives thanks to the five elements and silently closes her eyes and asks for her Great Aunt Sadie to come in, and anyone else, any guides to come. Doing ceremony with her mom amps up the intensity of the moment. She senses Great Aunt Sadie is standing right behind her as she pours the ashes from the beautiful vase into the waters of Lake Superior, burning the remnants of her hair and letting it go also.

She looks over her shoulder from her crouched position and sees her mom, her eyes closed, a smile around the corners of her mouth. In this light, Tessa swears she is seeing herself.

Her mother is so beautiful.

Tears spring to Tessa's eyes.

And so are you.

"And so am I," Tessa whispers. Some part of her is healing.

LATER THAT NIGHT, in the raucousness of a nearly full campground, Tessa and her mom enjoy s'mores over their campfire. They share a beer. Light banjo music comes from a few camp sites away. Long after they retire, the young men that were ingesting Jell-O shots in the site next door are yelling and banging.

They left their food out in bear country.

They're running around with iPhones and cameras, trying to chase the cubs.

Tessa flies out of the rig in an instant.

"Stop it!" she shouts, running in front of them and giving the cubs time to scramble away.

The three boys square off in front of her.

One of them sneers. "Who the fuck are you?"

"I'm camping next to you."

"So what?" One of them brushes aside her and she grips his arm with unyielding strength. Not letting go.

He tries to rip his arm away. "What the fuck?"

She releases him. She's trembling with barely controlled rage.

She sees the boy's fists ball up.

He rushes his face too close to hers, attempting to bully her backward, and she stays rooted to the earth. His alcohol breath circles them both like smoke from a fire.

"Are you even a girl?" He attempts a guttural and growling tone, but he's sloppy, weak, and drunk.

Suddenly he's yanked backward, feet off the ground, as if he's hit a live, electric line. An older guy with greying long hair and tattoos, has uprooted him unapologetically.

"Do what she says. Leave those cubs alone. Are you guys fucking idiots?"

A crowd has gathered. Moms and Dads and little kids, and Harley dudes and dudettes.

Everyone is intently looking at the three young men. Silently the crowd moves forward as one, like a wave, toward the now sheepish-looking boys. The three shrink back to their camp site.

“Fuck, we were just trying to get some pictures. They wrecked our food.”

“You wrecked your food,” a clean cut father says. His two kids, with big saucer eyes, watch him. “Put it up on a line between two trees, or stow it like the rest of us do. Where the cubs are, the mom is, and you’re endangering all of us by your stupidity.”

“Geez, quit acting like it’s a federal crime.”

“As a matter of fact it is.” A woman steps forward. “I’m a National Park Service law enforcement officer and what you’re doing violates a federal protection act. Would you like to push your luck?”

The boys, now quiet and out of F words, retreat to their camp.

“Didn’t think so.” The Harley guy grins. “And don’t bother these young ladies either.”

Tessa turns, her mom, in a robe, arms folded, is standing near her.

“Ladies.” The man tips his cap to them both. The crowd slowly disperses.

“Let us know if you have any trouble again,” someone calls to Tessa and her mom.

“Wow, baby.” Her mom encircles Tessa’s shoulders with her arm. “You are one powerful protector.”

Tessa smiles. Another piece of her is returning home.

CHAPTER 29

AS THEY DRIVE south over the Mackinaw Bridge, some parts of Tessa still tingle and rage over Dina's, "You could have kept . . . "

Angrily, Tessa tears the ring off her finger and tosses it out the open passenger window. The sun reflects a gleaming flash as the ring arcs over the green rail on its long journey to the bottom of Lake Michigan.

"Did you just do what I think you did?" Her mom, looking ahead as she drives, has a smile tipping the corner of her mouth.

"You're damn right I did."

They high five.

THEY MAKE CAMP in Lake Ann. Tessa wakes in the middle of the night, in the midst of nightmares. She wakes fearful and crying and in physical pain and nausea.

Her mom is a rock, awake and holding her. Murphy with both of them.

If this is her heart breaking wide open, why can't it just do it all at once?

What sense is grief?

Why is she being haunted?

What else is inside her, clawing for release?

Like a deer that has been shot but doesn't know its wound is mortal, it continues running, sometimes for miles. Tessa tapes her ankle snugly. She tries to run, not knowing if her internal wound will ever heal.

"Honey."

"Mom, I have to. I have to. It's the only thing, besides you being with me, keeping me sane."

She purposely chooses the hillier trail, by St. Mary's Lake. She gets as far as the curve all the way around the lake and she has to turn back. She limps, and it takes her twice as long to return as it did to run.

She nears the rig and sees Josh leaning against the pick-up truck, his one foot crossed over at the ankle.

He breaks into that beautiful smile of his as she half runs to him and sobs. She's never cried so much in her life.

"Now you and I do ceremony," he whispers into her hair.

"I have no more ashes . . ."

Tessa tries to block out the fight with Dina, she keeps her cheek against his chest and gazes down. He lifts her face up, thumbing her cheek. "Your eyes. We need to fix those."

Tessa changes into some long slacks and they drink tea with her mother.

They start for Josh's truck.

Tessa looks back. "C'mon, Murph."

But Murphy remains lying beside her mother and looks up.

"This is for you and me," Josh says.

At Pearl Lake he drives to the north side and pulls out the canoe.

Tessa follows his lead, and he holds the stern, while she slips up to the front, paddle in hand.

They cross beyond poison ivy point, past the eagles' nest. A loon calls from one of the other outlets—not an alarm cry, but the mournful evening song. Silently two sandhill cranes cross low and directly in front of them, red hues entering the light cirrus clouds above.

They're heading to the DNR primitive campsites. No official sites anywhere. No outhouses or drinking water, but the lake. A huge line of boulders prevents any traffic, save foot or horseback. One tent, a wisp of smoke rising from a cook campfire, sits in somber isolation. Two tall pine trees rise in silhouette against the darkening sunset sky.

Tessa wonders if this is their destination, why not just take the Rayle Road?

"You're always taking me the long way, Josh," she says.

Only his paddle stroke responds, slow, methodical, sure.

They pull up short of the lone camp.

A man crouches by the water. He stands and turns as they approach.

It's the monster.

His face is no longer half blood and he has no knife in his hands. In real life, he is not so tall anymore, and his eyes are filled with tears, though his head is mostly tilted down.

"Dad?"

Tessa is in disbelief.

He stands frozen, unable to move. He crosses his hands in front of him and his head barely nods.

"Wha—?"

Tessa turns to look for Josh, but he has receded, and she cannot spot him.

"What are you doing here?" She sinks down to one of the large boulders.

"I thought I killed you. I thought . . ." His voice is hoarse, as if he hasn't spoken in a very long time.

"I thought I killed you," Tessa says through her tears.

"You don't know how sorry I am." He looks away.

She's never seen her dad cry. But now his tears are falling just as fast as hers and still he doesn't approach.

Tessa holds out her hand. Some part of her is mortified she is doing this and the other part is just doing it.

He's there in an instant, a man child sobbing fully into her lap, muffled muted howling, "Please, forgive me."

She strokes his curly-topped head, like a mother to a child.

I will not hide my love as I do not hide my grief.

At some point, her father shifts and moves over to the water's edge, just a few feet away. He cups some of Pearl Lake in his hands.

The twilight is coming on rapidly now. A Michigan's autumn night quickening twilight. Tessa watches the now lavender light on the silhouette of his face, the curve of his cheeks, and his sanguine nose.

He pours the water over his face and offers her some.

She rises, takes a few steps, and crouches next to him. She reaches into the lake and washes her face.

"In the islands, in the Pacific, you have to ask permission for the water to let you in. There are four sets of waves and on the fourth, you follow her in. And when you leave, you always face her, asking permission to leave."

She doesn't know this father. What led to this? She has a million questions and yet she waits.

"You don't talk very much."

She shakes her head no.

She wishes Murphy was here. Her touchstone. His reactions would tell her everything.

"I took from you and Eli."

"Yourself." Her voice is soft. "You only took from you."

She doesn't say it harshly and she doesn't mean it that way. It simply is.

He accepts this with a nod.

"I learned that thou shalt not kill can also mean thou shalt not kill yourself. You never killed yourself for anyone. You never killed part of your soul. But I tried to make you do it. I killed part of my soul for others. For what they would think. I was so proud to have two boys. I was so proud to have you, who could climb anything, fearless, and fast and could see everything . . . and then, when you said you were really a girl . . . I didn't know what to do with that. What do I say, what do I feel when I tell all the guys? I felt God played a joke on me, for being so proud I had two sons."

They stand and she touches his scar, the deep groove she can't quite remember seeing herself create, yet remembers the heft of the ax in her hands and the sound it made when she connected. She remembers how it felt to stop the monster from killing her brother. She remembers how good it felt to know she saved her brother.

She moves her fingers gently over the partial ear, mostly hidden by his curly hair. "I did this to you. I remember it."

"You did this for Eli." He puts his hand over hers as she explores the healed wounds. "And I remember too."

"Uncle Chuck." Tessa suddenly freezes, fear rising.

Her father holds her hand calmly and together they count to four.

Her eyes widen. It is he who taught her to count to four, to be safe, to breathe, to wait.

"Chuck has his own demons." His voice allays her fear. "He has no business between you and me."

He touches his forehead to hers. Then, for the first time, they hug as equals.

In the dwindling light, over her father's shoulder, Tessa catches movement. She glimpses something pacing stealthily among the saplings.

A young doe is tiptoeing from the water's edge, her ears back, eyes avoiding contact. She walks silently, picking her way among the shore saplings and into the deeper woods, disappearing between the dusk of night and the forever.

Tessa closes her eyes and breathes, without counting.

Chris Convissor wants to live in a world where swimming like an otter, eating dark chocolate, laughing with loved ones and adventuring are respectable, self-funded activities. As a writer, she's been spotlighted in Grand Traverse Woman and Northern Express. She's also been featured in Labyris, A Room of One's Own (Vancouver, Canada) and her photography has appeared in St. Anthony's Press. When she's not inside writing about her imaginary friends, you can find her outside, working with her hands and adventuring.